The Amoeba-Ox Continuum

The Amoeba-Ox Continuum

Trent Portigal

Winchester, UK
Washington, USA

First published by Roundfire Books, 2017
Roundfire Books is an imprint of John Hunt Publishing Ltd., Laurel House, Station Approach,
Alresford, Hants, SO24 9JH, UK
office1@jhpbooks.net
www.johnhuntpublishing.com
www.roundfire-books.com

For distributor details and how to order please visit the 'Ordering' section on our website.

Text copyright: Trent Portigal 2017

ISBN: 978 1 78535 691 9
978 1 78535 692 6 (ebook)
Library of Congress Control Number: 2017932884

A CIP catalogue record for this book is available from the British Library.

Design: Stuart Davies

Printed and bound by CPI Group (UK) Ltd, Croydon, CR0 4YY, UK

We operate a distinctive and ethical publishing philosophy in
all areas of our business, from our global network of authors
to production and worldwide distribution.

Chapter 1

The square is blindingly white in the middle of the day. The buildings that frame it, also white, concentrate all the energy they can catch into the open expanse. A sliver of moon or the reflection of city lights off nighttime clouds is enough to read by. At the moment, the heat and light generated by this concentrated effort erases the individuality of the city hall and theatre on the long sides and the residential towers on the short sides. They become generic reflective surfaces, broken here and there by the relative blackness of occasional protrusions.

Natalie stands under one of the protrusions, indifferent to the role it plays in the articulation that, when visible, lends the building a certain elegance. Only the narrow shadow that it provides is important. She gazes into the square with squinted eyes, following the lingering blobs of what she takes to be tourists. She doubts that tourists are a common sight in the city, the somewhat obscure second city in the metropolitan area. Most people stick to the capital. She might of course be biased since, even as a lifelong resident of the capital, she has rarely ventured here. On the other hand, only tourists would be sufficiently caught up in the spectacle of the quarter to not notice that they are being slowly baked.

The blobs have ill-defined edges, as if the light and heat have already penetrated the outer layers and are starting to work on the still tender inner flesh. Somehow, the trees placed in meticulous rows in small pockets are clear and sharp, like surgical cuts in the light. They are thin; barely sticks with tufted tops. As far as Natalie knows, the square has been around for at least fifty years, so either the trees have found this environment less than ideal or they have been purposely replaced to offer only slight accents of color to the monotone space. Providing too much color, shade and perhaps habitat for small animals would have undoubtedly detracted from the purity of the original design.

She glances at her watch and then turns toward the face of the tower. Once her eyes adjust, she fishes a scrap of paper from her purse and enters the code scrawled on it into the intercom. A voice comes through a moment later: "Yes?"

"It's Natalie Chaulieu from the office, Mr. Andesmas. I am supposed to help you find your bearings."

"Good. I'll be down in a moment," the voice replies in a curt but not unpleasant tone.

Natalie continues to look toward the building so her eyes stay accustomed to the shade. She wants to scrutinize this mythical figure – according to others in the office, at any rate. The very fact that he has decided to stay here rather than live in the capital already sets him apart, as far as she is concerned; a politician purposely living farther away from the center of power than he needs to is unusual. Of course, as he is new in town, he could have just wandered here like the tourists in the square. If that is the case, the question becomes whether he has the sense to leave before he is cooked.

Her first glimpse, through the window beside the door, is of a grey man: dull, white, receding hair; worn face with features that fit together with a low-key sort of harmony; heavy, practical glasses; well-tailored suit without flash. He resembles the preferred model of a Committee member, probably having already been baked into the mold. He opens the door and passes without hesitation through the shadow into the light, motioning for her to follow him.

She pauses at the edge of the shadow as if it is a ledge overlooking an insubstantial mist, giving her eyes a moment to readjust and mentally putting a check in the senseless column. It's hard to imagine that he can even see where he is going, even if he hasn't yet run into anything. Senseless he may be, but not to the point of self-destruction. And, grey he may be in ordinary circumstances, but not in this light. He seems to absorb the energy, making his hair shine and his skin's appear robust rather than decayed. Even his suit gains a subtle sheen, as if channeling the energy through special threads woven into the fabric. As she hurries to catch up, she wonders if the check in the senseless column wasn't too hasty.

"It doesn't seem like you need showing around," she comments once she is beside him. "Have you been here before?"

"No. I wandered around yesterday, though. You?" They walk around the edge of the square toward the opening between the city hall and a tower.

"Once or twice. If one doesn't live or work here, there isn't much reason to come. I mean, the Towers is unique, but not an attraction per se."

"Good thing that the office sent you, then."

"The others were worse; most of them had never even heard of the place. I see why you chose it, though."

"I doubt that."

"Okay."

"Why did you come, the one or two times you were here?"

"Picking up dirty laundry, a job during high school. It's weird. I actually went to the industrial districts more often than here. Maybe the people here are all impossibly immaculate, like the square."

"The reason you thought I chose this place?"

"That was the general idea, yes."

"I suppose that is flattering."

"Sure."

"Particularly since all this really exists, no matter how impossible it may seem." Andesmas stops and gestures at the buildings. "A utopia at scale, built before the war, before the Committee existed. It is the crystallization of the ingenuity of workers—of cooperation—right in front of us."

"My utopia has more shade."

"This utopia has plenty of shade, on the other side of city hall. There's color too, which might or might not be immaculate."

"Whether you have been here before or not, you seem to know the city pretty well."

"I don't know this city. Feeling the energy of the place is enough."

"Like Hiroshima."

"I don't understand the connection."

"It's nothing. Well, when we reach the decidedly maculate capital, I should be able to be of more help."

"You do know that that is not the reason you were chosen?"

"Yes, but I'd prefer being useful all the same."

"I would expect no less. Your mother was a remarkable woman."

"I think you mean 'is' a remarkable woman."

A smile flashes across Andesmas's face. "Your mother was a remarkable judge."

"And my father was a remarkable novelist."

"You are basing the opinion on personal experience?"

Natalie counts to ten before answering, "In the same way that yours is, I imagine."

She then bites her tongue before adding *you hypocritical fuck.*

"You know why I was asked to join the Committee?"

"Politics at that level is none of my business."

"But you know, nonetheless."

"I don't recall."

"Fair enough. I am here to repair the damage done to our country's reputation by the dissemination of a charter a couple of years ago now. You, of course, don't know anything about the document."

"I am shocked to hear that such a charter exists."

"It was written and signed by some otherwise remarkable members of our society at the time, your mother—your parents—included. Their choice made it clear that they no longer desired to be part of society; to continue the constructive dialogue toward a better future. Perhaps it was just impatience that led to the decision. Impatience leads to a great many bad decisions. It is important, though, to react to those decisions in a constructive way.

"For instance, the demonstrations fifteen-odd years ago were more than anything an expression of youthful exuberance. People weren't unhappy with the direction society was going, just the sacrifices needed to get there coupled with a lack of discernable progress. Tanks in the streets as a response was very successful in shutting them down in the short term, but the risk aversion that went along with it slowed progress even further—sometimes to the point of regression. So, the sacrifices continued, impatience built up over time, and BAM.

"I can never know the Towers. I can, however, still feel the optimism, the effort and the sacrifice that resulted in this concrete example of progress in our society. That is the direction of the Committee, that is the message that needs to be spread, and that is what the charter threatens to undermine."

"And the tanks?"

"They are a tool that can be useful under certain circumstances. These are not those circumstances. Regretfully, we have had to separate some of the people from society physically, since it was not enough for them to declare that they no longer wished to participate in our common project. They wished to actively undermine it, regardless of the harm that would cause everyone else. I am sure that you don't know anyone like that."

"No one comes to mind."

"Of course."

"Where are we going?" Natalie asks, realizing that she is no better than the tourists, Andesmas or the proverbial frog, standing as she is in the square.

"To a cabaret, ominously named the Cabaret of the Three Caskets. It is more of a café at this hour."

The two start walking again, slowly.

"Anyway," Andesmas continues, "this is an opportunity for you. No matter how misguided the actions of your parents were—whether you personally think they were misguided or not—they did want something positive for our country. That is why I mentioned the work your mother did when she was a judge, despite your obvious sensitivity to it. She spent a great deal of time moving our common project forward. We shouldn't lose sight of that. And, we shouldn't deprive you of the opportunity to do the same. Instead, we will make sure that you are in a position to see firsthand the improvements that we are making on a daily basis.

"It won't be as brilliant as the Towers, though with your energy and intelligence working in concert with so many others we might as well be that ambitious."

"It sounds like you have everything planned out."

"I don't, which you will learn very quickly. There is no point in dwelling on what we don't know and can't predict. Better to spend one's time bringing good people together—and you are a good person—and do the best we can with our resources."

"I would say that I can tell why the Committee is bringing you on, but you'd probably say that I am wrong or missing the point."

"Why don't you explain before I decide."

"You have painted a pretty compelling picture of the future of the common project, all the while being very careful to manage expectations. You offer a rallying cry that one could say is badly needed; optimistic without falling into naïveté."

"That is once again flattering. Thank you. If my voice can be useful to our society, then I will lend it to the Committee. And I haven't proven to you yet that I am more than that voice. I am no empty shirt, figurehead, or whatever else might come to mind, though all you get for now is words. What I propose is that we turn these words into action together. I propose that you make a more constructive choice than your parents, who, despite their many merits, decided in the end to no longer participate, to limit themselves to criticizing our country from the skewed perspective of the sidelines."

Natalie counts to ten. "So I would assist you in all this?"

"You would assist the Committee, but would lead projects and have significant autonomy."

"I would leave the office?"

"For the moment, you will still be based out of the office."

"No more pretending to show people from out of town around?"

"I wouldn't rule it out. After all, the future is unknown. I am curious to discover your maculate capital. I imagine that it is not the side of the city I am used to seeing."

"Probably not."

"Although I am supposedly the guest, the coffee is on me."

The two enter the cabaret.

"I didn't ask yesterday," Andesmas says, addressing the server behind the counter, "why is this place called the Cabaret of the Three Caskets?"

"It is famous for being Death's favorite watering hole."

Andesmas looks around at the walls as white as the square, brightly colored in places where the light filters through stained glass windows cut in abstract patterns. He then looks questioningly at Natalie, who shrugs.

"This doesn't seem to be the sort of place that Death would feel welcome," Andesmas says.

"I don't think she cared, only coming in to get blind drunk."

"'She'?"

"Force of habit; could have been a 'he', hard to tell with Death."

"So you have met Death?"

"Not personally, no. I would probably have to be dead for that."

"You talk as if you are familiar with, well, her, though."

"It is her favorite watering hole."

"Right. What does she like to drink?"

"Blood."

"Of course. You have a lot of that on hand?"

"Nah, it is a quick fermentation of the freshly dead, best brought in locally right before she hits town."

"Do you have a recipe?"

"Not as such. There are notes scrawled on the vats, though."

"Why don't you make some and offer it to other customers? It sounds like a house specialty."

"It is one thing to be welcoming when Death comes to town, another to give her an additional reason to be here."

"Ah. And how do you know when she is going to come to town?"

"The trail of dead heading in this direction."

"Of course."

"It hasn't been as clear-cut in the last fifty years or so. There have been a lot more isolated incidents; an industrial accident here, a train derailment there, a building that collapses across town. It was easier when it was just disease and war."

"Even disease and war are probably harder to track these days."

"That is offset by better techniques and communication. Try to imagine the technical chaos before Pasteur and the ignorance before telephones, telegraphs, televisions, tele-whatevers."

"I'll give you Pasteur, though the tele-whatevers are just as good at spreading misinformation as facts."

"The misinformation is usually focused on the 'why' and 'how' of the dead, not the fact that people are dead."

"Sometimes, sometimes not. Wait, this means that the cabaret has been here longer than the Towers."

"In roughly the same place."

"When Death was here then, this place was probably dark and desolate. When was she here last?"

"I don't know specifically."

"The caskets mean something?"

"They represent the three major plagues that swept through the town."

"The cabaret was probably the only watering hole at that time, known already for its alcohol and excess. So, of course, when everybody started dying, it made sense for them to see Death as drunk and out of control. I bet that, if the local priest survived, he used it as an excuse to preach temperance."

"You are taking Death as a personification of death."

"Yes. I am not making light of it, or her. I'm sure that those times were horrifying and that considering death as a person was a way to cope, to not feel so helpless. And that was before Pasteur and so many other advancements. They had no idea what was going on."

"Death was a superstition, then."

"There is a reason why the name didn't change to four caskets after the flu epidemic, six after the wars, and so on. It is useful for us to hold on to those traditions, those memories, so we are aware of how far we have come. It is instructive to know that the Towers was built on a benighted town and not *ex nihilo*."

"I don't think that Death is just a superstition. If she was, why would we have the vats and notes?"

"That is a worthwhile research project. It is not a reason to jump to irrational conclusions. I'll have a coffee. Natalie?"

"Lemon tea and a half-pint of top-fermented blood, please."

The server hesitates before Andesmas states flatly, "She is joking. In bad taste."

"Coppery," Natalie says. "I wouldn't say bad so much as acquired. According to Death, it's worth the effort."

"I am not sure which is worse," the server mutters as he prepares the drinks, "saying that Death does not exist or making jokes at her expense."

"Where does immortality fit into your plan for a better future?" Natalie asks Andesmas.

"Nowhere."

"Not even under theoretical research?"

"It is not a Committee priority. If scientists believe that it is worth pursuing, they are free to do so."

"I guess we should be respectful of Death at least until we can live forever."

"I was being respectful."

"Calling her an outdated superstition?"

"An important tradition that we should rationally be aware of."

"A tradition that does nothing but show how backwards we once were."

"Correct. It is not constructive to believe that Death will come walking through the door, get drunk on fermented blood and then start killing people left and right. That would be counter to the common project."

The server puts the two cups on the counter, along with a receipt on a third saucer. He clearly wants to say more, but stays silent. Andesmas checks the temperature of the coffee, and then, once he has confirmed that it is drinkable, downs it quickly. Natalie, after thanking the server, waits while her tea steeps. A look of impatience flashes across Andesmas's face, disappearing before anyone notices it.

"The story then is that Death comes to town with the plague," Andesmas summarizes aloud to distract himself. "She gets drunk and kills people; gets drunker, kills more people. Then, eventually, she moves on and it's time to bury the dead. That's it?"

"There's more," the server replies. "Townspeople try to reason with her, beg her to stop or just take them and not their children. Then the Virgin Mary and Jesus ask her to have mercy on the people, but she is too far gone to listen. Some have the idea of catching her before she arrives with gifts of food and wine, so she would be too full for blood, but she is still feeling the effects of the blood from the last town and is already thirsty for more. She doesn't pay attention, but I guess they have to try."

Andesmas nods without listening. "That is not how to make tea," he says to Natalie, "if you steep it any longer it will be ruined."

"Noted." She continues to let it steep.

He takes a spoon, leans over, fishes the teabag out of the cup, and puts it on the edge of the saucer in the same unwavering manner as when he walked from the shadow into the light in the square. She looks at the tea, blinks, then turns to him and says:

10

"You have to be in the capital for a meeting with the other members of the Committee in half an hour. We should go."

She steps away from the counter, waits for him to pay. When they are back in the street, she thanks him for the tea and they head to the metro station.

Chapter 2

After her impertinence in the cabaret, Natalie does not expect to hear from Andesmas again. He was undoubtedly looking for someone sufficiently compliant and cowed—yet energetic and bright—to join his secular crusade. It would have been a feather in his cap to have someone who, on top of those qualities, was the daughter of signatories of the dreaded charter. It was clear, looking back, that he had arranged the whole thing; a rousing discourse about a glorious future in the middle of a still brilliant workers' paradise of old. She imagines him putting extra gel in his hair and choosing that one suit that would make him shine as soon as he stepped into the intense light of the square. He was more than just a highly regarded politician called in to save the day and move the Committee past the shadow of the charter, on which it has been stuck for several years. He had an intimate connection to the brilliance, to the broader ideas that the Committee was supposed to champion.

He had probably thought that she was an easy target, as she was already working in the central government office doing menial tasks for bureaucrats several layers below the Committee. If she had already compromised to that extent, why wouldn't she want to do more interesting work in exchange? Of course, if Andesmas was genuine, he wouldn't see it as a compromise at all. By doing nothing, he was already fulfilling his promise of having her be part of something bigger; of progress, a better society in the making and all that. So long as one believes that the Committee is heading in the right direction, rather than being a clueless navigator of a ship of fools. The ship of fools sounds far more amusing to Natalie than striving for the shiny bauble in Andesmas's mind's eye and no more doomed to failure.

She would like clothes with the magic thread so that she could disguise her true nature and lose herself in the light. Every morning she has been capable of coherent and complex thought for the past six months, she has promised herself that she will go shopping for something brilliant. Then she has randomly chosen articles from her wardrobe, knowing that everything she owns that is appropriate for work makes her look like an apprentice grey man. If she was particularly coherent, she asked herself the eternal question of why "man" comes to mind first, when "amoeba" was far more appropriate, and why "grey" rather than "insipid." Once or twice a month, she made it to the mundane conclusion that it probably had to do with the number of syllables more than anything else. She has nonetheless promised herself to use the more accurate expression if the appropriate circumstances arise.

It is not as if nothing happened for six months. The direction, beyond making sure that the trains run on time, is to release a competing charter, with its own set of high-profile signatories. The challenge with high-profile people is that they have a red file as thick as they are important. If they need to be taken down a notch or ten with some credibility, the Committee needs a great deal of ammunition. Possessing an illegal book may be enough for an ordinary citizen to be sent away for a while; an illegal library is required to do the same to a citizen who has an international reputation. Someone has to go through the file and create two plans; one detailing the most effective enticements to convince them to sign the document, and another to manage any potentially embarrassing revelations after they are linked to the Committee's position. Natalie's group is responsible for writing plans for filler candidates, who are on the whole a bland bunch. It is important to have more signatures than the old charter, even if that means scraping the bottom of the high-profile barrel. Anyone can be high profile if the population is narrowed to niches and specialties.

Today's VIP is a professor at The National School of Puppetry by the name of Tonda Keller. Natalie did not know that the country had a school of puppetry. In other circumstances, she would likely be interested to know about this star of the classical marionette world. As it stands, by the third time she has read his mercifully light file, cataloguing every reason for him to sign whatever the Committee might put in front of him, she curses his middle-of-the-road, utterly relative genius. The poor sap's life is about to be turned upside down because he happens to be less mediocre than the people around him, and she can't help herself for wanting it. She wagers that a threat to cancel his puppetry guild membership and to transfer him to pretty much any position away from the art he loves would be more than enough to push him in the appropriate direction. It would serve him right for caring that much.

As soon as she has typed up the reports and the file has been put on the finished pile, she feels exhausted. She starts to put on her coat—the need to get out, drink whatever she happened to put in her flask is the only motivation that is able to make it through to her consciousness—when an office automaton from higher up the chain clears his throat and says in an upbeat tone: "You must be Natalie Chaulieu."

She jumps, having no idea that anyone was standing by her desk. She looks hard at him for a moment, before replying, "And you are the very picture of an insipid amoeba."

The man blinks several times, clearly having difficulty processing what she said.

"Artistic license, it's a Committee priority," she explains, before nodding toward a small meeting room at the edge of the open plan office. "If you want to discuss something . . ."

The man nods.

"Is there a file in particular you are interested in?"

"No," he says, finally finding his voice.

"Okay."

She leads the way to the office, leaving her coat and any thoughts of escape behind. When they have taken a seat and the door is closed, she waits for him to begin. He takes an envelope out of his briefcase and lays it on the table.

"I would like to say that I admire the work your mother did in keeping our society on the right path for so long."

Natalie counts to ten.

"Right, well, I work with Mr. Andesmas. We all work with Mr. Andesmas, of course. The work you are doing is very important in helping the Committee get the right message out. Your mother would be proud, I have no doubt."

"You think so, I mean really think so?"

"Yes, of course."

"Because that is all that I've ever wanted. It's just been so hard to live up to her example."

"You are doing a great job."

"What with the Committee deciding that I shouldn't be allowed to go to university."

"I-I don't know anything about that."

"She was such a direct influence on me, especially after being sent off to a job endlessly wandering the prairies."

"Doing important work, I'm sure."

"It's just so sad that she's gone forever."

"But she, uh, okay, let's get back to the subject at hand."

"I am just not sure that I can concentrate. Please, give me a moment."

"Um."

"It's just so nice to meet someone who appreciated her. So, so nice."

A long, awkward pause follows.

"As, as I mentioned, I am working with Mr. Andesmas . . ."

"It must be very rewarding working for him," Natalie cuts in.

"Yes, it . . ."

"I met him once."

"Well, that's . . ."

"A brilliant and purposeful man, if I may say so."

"Yes, he . . ."

"It is so uplifting to know that a man like that is steering the boat."

The man stays silent.

"How long have you been working with him?"

"About six months."

"Do you find it rewarding?"

"Yes, of course."

"He must have seen something special in you. He is really very perceptive."

The man can only manage a nervous laugh.

"Tell me, what do you find the most rewarding?"

"I . . . It's hard to say. Everything we do is so important in making our society better."

"What's in the envelope?"

"What? Oh right, so Mr. Andesmas . . ."

"Why don't you lay the contents out on the table? I am supposed to see them, right?"

"Yes, okay, sure." He pulls out a small stack of letters and spreads them out between them.

"Mr. Andesmas?"

"Right, well, he evidently thinks very highly of you too, and so—"

"Really? That's so flattering."

"So, he wanted to task you with a sensitive project—"

"Let me guess, a potential signatory who needs special treatment."

"No."

"A draft of the charter he wants to spruce up."

He shakes his head.

"A foreign dignitary is coming into town. Mr. Andesmas probably has fond memories of when I helped him find his bearings in the capital. The man is a genius, but, between you and me, he couldn't find north with a compass."

"Just, just read the letters!" He pushes the letters toward her side of the table.

"It's probably the tall buildings; that's what usually throws people from the countryside."

Natalie scans the letters as she talks. When she is done, she looks up with incredulity.

"So, as you can see," the man says after a pause, "a delicate situation."

"Seafood?"

"Well, yes."

"Don't we have food inspectors for this sort of thing? I mean, if bad mussels are killing people, there should be a whole agency to take care of it."

"Yes, there is. The seafood is not killing people."

"Because I know nothing about rotten food."

"We are aware of that."

"I can barely cook."

"Yes."

"So, what's the job?"

"We need to know what is killing people."

"Not really an expert there either."

"Yes. You will act as the liaison to the Committee on this. You will be working with a professional on the ground, but we need a direct link to the investigation, someone who understands the city and is aware of the politics."

"Dead people aren't good for the Committee's image?"

"The people don't matter. I mean, they do matter; they matter a great deal. They're just not politically important. Or, rather, at any rate, for the central government. It's up to the agencies, as you said, to take care of ordinary incidents, mortalities. It's the international side of what's going on that you will be focusing on."

"The seafood."

"Yes. We are a landlocked country. Seafood is imported as part of broad agreements with our neighbors. Implying that the seafood is bad is not great for our relations with them."

"Especially with the new charter around the corner."

"The charter is not relevant."

"If you say so. What if it turns out that the mussels are the cause?"

"It is highly unlikely. People stopped eating seafood a month ago and the incidents have continued. The seafood is still blamed, but only because nothing definitive has turned up."

"Where is the outbreak?"

"The Towers. You'll be . . ."

"Ha! It's Death."

The man blinks, and then gives Natalie a look as if she has gone off the deep end.

"Mr. Andesmas knows this," she continues. "Death comes around The Towers once in a while to get tanked on blood and kill a pile of people. It's a vicious circle since she needs more corpses to keep drinking, which just makes her thirstier. Eventually she moves on though, just have to be patient. Case solved!"

"I don't, no, that's not . . . Mr. Andesmas can't believe; just don't say anything about Death, I mean, like, an individual, when you are out there. Just find the facts, follow the lead of the expert, report back to me. Don't assume anything. People are already panicked. Don't add to it. Please."

"What would happen if people just stopped liking seafood, found it slimy and were repulsed by most of it being bottom-feeders? Wouldn't the effect be the same?"

"Unless it happened overnight, no. And, nobody would be saying that eating it would kill you."

"Fair points."

"You are going to be meeting"—the man refers to notes scribbled on the envelope—"André Monnier at . . ." He double-checks. "The Cabaret of the Three Caskets. Odd name for a cabaret, odd to meet in a cabaret."

"Really? Mr. Andesmas isn't just trying to screw with me?"

"Mr. Andesmas is above reproach. How you are acting, it is hard to believe that anyone would entrust you with . . . but, no, Mr. Andesmas sees something in you, too. You are to meet Mr. Monnier at eight o'clock. Please be professional; you are representing the Committee."

He gets up to leave, pauses as if he has something more to say, thinks better of it, and then exits the room.

Natalie sits for a while, contemplating whether she should profit from being in the room to take a nip from her flask. Then she sighs, gathers up the letters without looking at them and stuffs them back in the envelope. Making the amoeba feel uncomfortable was fun and certainly took her mind off Keller and all the other victims she was setting up for the government. She can't decide whether she is one of them are not. Going back to the cabaret can't just be a coincidence, but it makes no sense for Andesmas to go to any more effort on her account.

Screw it, she concludes. *It gets me out of the office, away from the files.*

She takes a sip, then another. After, she goes back to her desk, the weight of judging the next VIP slowing her down more and more with each step.

Chapter 3

"It's typhoid," André states as Natalie sits down at the only occupied table in the cabaret.

"Ah, brilliant. So, we are done here? I can go? I mean, maybe I should stay for a while, just to be sure. We wouldn't want to rush anything."

She looks at the steady stream of men—effectively amoebas—who come in, order a coffee at the counter, drink it as soon as it arrives with a practiced gesture, leave a coin or two and walk out. Three men lean against the counter at one end, nursing their drinks.

André takes his time before responding: "Whatever you think is best."

She focuses on him, deciding that he doesn't quite fit the amoeba mold. After some reflection, she concludes that he is more like an old ox who has spent his life slowly dragging a plow across a field.

"I have to say that I am sort of disappointed to not see Death at the bar when I came in," she continues.

"Death would be going thirsty if she was here."

"Wait, nobody's died?"

"A handful, those too far gone for treatment."

"And you know the story of Death? Right, stupid question. You're here, of course you know the story. Are you a doctor?"

He slowly shakes his head.

She looks at him questioningly until he finally opens his mouth. "Health inspector, of sorts."

Finding that her enthusiasm is already flagging, Natalie goes to order a tea at the counter. She then settles in to wait for her ox to do his thing. She can follow him, take notes as needed and report on whatever seems appropriate. If Andesmas wants her to do this, she'll play along for now.

Leaving the cabaret, she remarks that her ox, while moving forward at his lumbering pace, focuses his attention on the sky. It is another beautiful, sunny day; the sky a pale shade of blue that seems rich in contrast to the white buildings that frame it.

"A good day to avoid the square," she says.

He does not respond to her comment. They head, in any case, in the opposite direction, to an apartment building at the edge of the Towers. They are buzzed in, and find themselves in a lobby that someone seems to put a lot of effort into keeping white, if the faint paint smell is any indication, but has never quite succeeded. Natalie can't decide whether it's the light, or whether the walls themselves have a slightly yellowish grey tint. A woman is standing off to the side, organizing medical equipment on a wooden bench and placing it in her satchel. She wears the grey uniform, but on her, it comes off more like cinders than mediocrity. Natalie wants to find a poker and stir them to see if there are live embers underneath.

André shifts direction and the two of them approach her.

"André," the woman says, looking up at them.

"Helen," he replies, obviously not feeling the need to introduce Natalie.

"Stupid."

André nods. "Yup."

Natalie decides to prod. "Stupid? How so?"

Helen looks at her clinically before responding. "You don't look well."

"I feel great."

Helen turns back to the bench and finishes packing her instruments. "Probably should drink less."

"I'm fairly sure that nobody asked for your opinion on the subject."

Helen shrugs with the same fatigued manner as André, picks up her freshly repacked bag and walks toward the exit. Just before the door, she turns back to André to say, "You'll have the files tomorrow." Then, she is gone.

Natalie realizes only when she and André are alone that her question hadn't been answered.

"What did she mean by 'stupid'?" she asks André, without much hope for an articulate response.

"It's stupid that people are dying of typhoid fever here and now." He walks to the elevator and pushes the button.

"Right, but why?"

"It's not something one dies of in this day and age, at least not around here."

The elevator comes and takes them to the eighth floor. Natalie figures that it makes more sense to find a book on the subject rather than to keep asking ignorant questions, so she makes a mental note and reverts to following André silently.

As they walk down the hallway, André fills her in on the situation.

"We are going to inspect the household of one of the victims and ask his mother some questions. Single mother, two sons; five and nine. The five-year-old died."

Natalie nods and steels herself against her repulsion of invading people's intimate, emotionally charged spaces. She is distracted by the stained-glass window at the end of the hallway, similar to the one at the cabaret. She is sure that the walls are just as yellow-grey as the ones in the lobby, but the bright colors projected on them from the window make them look perfectly white. She remembers Andesmas's comment about this not being the sort of place that Death would frequent, and finds herself agreeing. *Yet*, she thinks to herself, *here we are.*

The woman who answers the door makes André seem gay and spritely. She doesn't bother confirming who they are, just leaves the door open so they can follow her through a cluttered living room into the kitchen. She sits at the table, so André and Natalie follow her lead. Natalie fidgets in the awkward silence, trying to look and not look at everything around her at the same time. Both André and the woman, undoubtedly the mother, seem comfortable marinating in their own thoughts and emotions.

After noticing a kettle on the stove, Natalie starts to ask the woman if she can make tea. Then she decides that it would be better to just do it, so she jumps up and puts the kettle on. She also mentally notes that she needs to ask André the names of people before they enter. The cabinets stand closed in front of her, the yellow-grey overwhelming any sense of white they might once have had. Tea and cups are on the other side of the opaque doors, but so is intimacy: she imagines a variety of cups gathered over the years, linked to events, memories; a chamomile blend that the mother's grandmother used to prepare to warm the cold, scary nights when the mother was a child. The tea's magic has probably been lost, replaced by a crushing sense of impotence against a disease that never should have made its way into this discolored utopia. What if Natalie opens a cabinet and this weight escapes, settles on this woman who barely has the strength to hold herself upright.

"Why him?" the mother whispers, barely loud enough to be heard over the heating water. "It should have taken me."

The kettle starts to whistle, at first weakly but quickly with increasing insistence. It hits Natalie, waking her from her reverie. She hurriedly searches for what she needs, closing the doors as soon as she can. She only notices that she is slamming the doors and that the kettle has hit an ear-splitting pitch when she glances back at the table and sees both André and the mother staring at her; the first in detached curiosity, the second in muted horror. She turns red at the realization, takes the kettle off the burner, puts random teabags in each cup and pours the water. Her hold on the kettle puts her hand in the path of the rising steam, but she ignores it, concentrating on pouring into the cups and stopping before they overflow. Not being able to hold the kettle any longer, she lets it fall back on the stove. Finally, she carries the cups to the table, leaving rings on the counter. When she sits down again, she mumbles an apology.

"'Why him?' is the question we hope to answer," André says.

"You and Theo were not sick?"

"No."

"So, what did Albert do that neither of you did? It is helpful to run through a day, starting with products he may have used in the morning, what he had for breakfast, and so on. Why don't we start in his bedroom?"

The mother nods and gets up with more energy than she has shown up until this point. André follows her to the bedroom, while Natalie stays at the table, looking at the untouched tea. After a moment, she quietly follows them. She stares at André's back and ignores what they are saying so as to feel slightly more comfortable about being in the apartment. She gets the sense that she is walking down a narrow tunnel insulated from the noise of the surface, yet illuminated with enough phosphorescent algae for the world to still be somewhat open. Only André, the end of the tunnel, is somber and grey. That, in Natalie's opinion, would suit a walk toward Death, if she was still lurking in the bedroom. It would make sense; a five-year-old could not offer much blood, but his death would attract so many others to this conveniently small room. Then she would have the fresh and tasty blood from the child to start and copious amounts of older, less appetizing blood when the taste no longer mattered. Natalie is not entirely sure why Death would need to bother with such cleverness; maybe she was just adapting to a faster moving and more skeptical modern world.

Natalie's train of thought is interrupted by what she first takes as flashes of more colorful algae off to the side. She continues to walk, bumping into André. He doesn't react, no doubt saying something to the mother that Natalie barely registers. She mumbles another apology without taking her eyes off the wall, which slowly comes into focus. The wall is covered up to the height of her shoulders with crude drawings in all the colors of the rainbow. She thinks that most of them are squirrels but can't be sure. The thought from the hallway returns: *this is not a place for Death.*

She wants to kick herself for being taken in by such a naive idea.

24

Hospitals are painted in light colors and are flooded with light. The dying are often surrounded by bright flowers, themselves more often than not living on borrowed time in their water-filled vases. Then there are the cards and whatever else visitors can think of to enliven the space. André's dark grey form represents, if anything, the plodding perseverance of life. He is no different from the life of the maculate capital that needs mundane services like laundries. She smiles at her tendency to just flip broad generalizations, only sprinkling on enough nuance to hide their superficiality.

"At first it was just the flu. I mean, we thought it was the flu. He had a fever . . ."

As Natalie stares at the wall, wondering why squirrels was the first idea that jumped into her head, she finds the conversation between the mother and André seeping into her tunnel. It is not so much a conversation as a monologue about the sickness, irrelevant to the question André asked. The mother might have already detailed what Albert did that was different from the rest of the family, but Natalie can't be sure. In any case, André seems to be patiently listening. Perhaps he thinks that some additional information might be revealed, perhaps he is just being considerate.

". . . It was when he started staring at the drawings, as if nothing else in the world existed. And clutching at nothing. He would just grasp air, slowly, carefully . . ."

The words trail off. Natalie turns to the mother, who is sitting on the bed, mimicking her son's movements. They resemble those of a lizard on a cold day.

"What are the drawings of?" Natalie asks hurriedly, needing to know more yet wanting to reestablish as quickly as possible whatever distance she can manage from this woman's tragedy.

The question takes the mother by surprise. She stops grasping the air and looks at the wall as if it had just appeared after a long absence. "It's the coronation of King Squirrel the First. Theo was going to draw all the great moments in his reign. At dinner, we would talk about their ongoing war against the soulless dinosaurs, the Olympic games of shiny objects. . . It was of no use to ask how school was going or anything else. I don't know where they got all those ideas. Albert was so full of imagination."

"They are all squirrels?" Natalie asks without looking back.

"Oh, no. Just the king. Maybe a couple of others. I don't know, don't remember. I'm a terrible mother. I didn't pay enough attention. If I had only taken him to the hospital earlier . . ."

The room falls into silence. Natalie once again has to fight the urge to run away. She pushes the last words of the mother to the back of her mind and concentrates on figuring out which figure on the wall is the king, all the while repeating to herself that there is no point regretting questions asked.

"Why don't we go to the bathroom, we can go through what he did to get ready in the morning and before he went to bed?" André suggests gently.

Natalie hears the mother get up and the two leave the room. She follows them out, skipping from looking at the wall to André. Instead of turning toward the bathroom, she heads to the safe haven, relatively speaking, of the kitchen. She cleans up the spilled water on the counter, empties the kettle and puts the boxes of tea back where she found them. She is exaggeratedly careful when opening and closing the cabinets and setting down the kettle to make as little noise as possible. The desire to scrub all the surfaces to get rid of the yellow-grey tint takes hold. She shakes her head; even if it were possible to uncover the original pure white, it will have erased nothing. Instead, she turns to the table and contemplates the untouched cups of tepid, over-steeped tea. Before she has a chance to decide whether she should wash them as well, she hears the mother and André approach.

". . . like green gravy, and he would have to go ten times a day. When we had to carry him — it was so easy, he weighed nothing at all — I took him to the hospital. Too late, it was just too late. If only I could have taken his place."

The two enter the kitchen and take the same places at the table.

Natalie decides to ignore the cups and join them. She doesn't want to do anything with an audience and risk making an even bigger fool of herself. She feels that she can manage pretending to listen and be sympathetic without screwing it up. The worst would be to hear too much, but that would only be miserable for her; something she can live with.

"Before that, he was still going to school?" André asks.

"Kindergarten, yes. Until he started feeling sick."

"Did anyone go with him?"

"He always wanted to go with his brother. It never bothered Theo, to have his little brother around."

"Theo is at school now?"

The mother nods. "I could have kept him home longer, but then . . . I mean, I should go back to work, I just can't . . . If only I had taken him to the hospital sooner."

"He goes to the local school?"

The mother nods again.

"Thank you for going through this with me. I can't imagine how hard it was. It will help us in putting a stop to the outbreak."

André takes his leave with Natalie in tow. When they are in the elevator, Natalie asks: "Why didn't you tell her it wasn't her fault?"

"I am not the one to judge."

"Sure, but that kind of misses the point. It would just make her feel better."

André doesn't reply.

"So, now what? We go to the school?"

"No."

They sink into silence until they reach the street. André once again scans the sky, which makes absolutely no sense to Natalie. Even though they are not in the square, the angle of the sun makes the street almost as blinding. Looking up is rewarded by flashes of color that look like the court of the Squirrel King come to life.

As much as she would like to just turn off her brain and follow

André like an automaton, numb to the weight of people's experiences, she has to admit to herself that she is clearly incapable of actually doing it. With enough practice, maybe she would do better, but she doesn't imagine that she will be doing this sort of thing for much longer. In a month or two at most, she will most likely be back in the office with a pile of files to keep her company. Of course, she will be just as happy if invading people's homes never becomes as easy for her as leafing through the paper version of their lives.

"Right, so I made a bit of a mess in there," Natalie says. "I apologize for that. I know that I am just a hanger-on imposed by the Committee that you would rather do without. I mean, I wouldn't want someone like me on my back all the time. Happily, it is just for this case, or file, or whatever you call it. So, if only so I don't step on your toes or screw things up in the future, how's about you let me in a bit more on what we're doing. You don't need to tell me everything, just enough so I am not going in blind. Okay?"

"Fine."

Natalie waits a moment for André to continue. When he doesn't, she asks, "Why aren't we going to the school?"

"Theo's not there. The doctors already went through to test everyone. Helen will be bringing the files tomorrow."

"How do you know that Theo's not there?"

"The same way that I knew his mother would be home. I called ahead."

"What do we do now?"

"I have a meeting on another file. You can do what you like."

"What do I tell the Committee?"

"It's typhoid fever. The local population has been informed. Tests and vaccinations have been performed as per standard protocol. No general announcements should be made until the source is found."

"I'm comfortable with that."

"So much the better."

"When do we meet tomorrow?"

"I should have the files between eight and nine."

"At the Caskets?"

André nods.

"Okay, good. I'll see you tomorrow. I am pretty good with files; I will be able to be more useful."

André grimaces and then walks off in his plodding gait.

André as the plodding perseverance of life. Natalie decides that she wishes that she could just ask for his file, next time she is in the office. It would be easier than trying to get to know him personally. The priority, though, is to find out more about the disease. Happily, events have conspired to give her the rest of the day to spend at the library.

Chapter 4

"Why are we even here?" George grumbles. "There are plenty of places to go closer to home."

"It's good to get out of the capital once in a while," Natalie responds.

"We aren't in the capital? When did we leave the capital? It all looks the same to me."

"That's what I love about you; your keen sense of observation."

"Laugh it up. Any other guy would have left you long ago, using 'love' as an insult all the time."

"Well, aren't we grumpy."

"Yes, we are grumpy. You would be too if you had to drive out to some town in the middle of nowhere every day to film how so-called real people live. And then, instead of just going out to someplace nice and local and easy with my girlfriend, I'm dragged to some random place for some mysterious reason. All I have to say is that the surprise had better be good, with someplace to sit and something to eat."

"But the people are nice."

"What?"

"The people in that little town in the middle of nowhere."

"They're lovely people, salt of the earth."

"You could stay out there during the shoot, you know."

"And miss your sarcastic rendition of 'love'?"

"It isn't that long, and I'm not going anywhere."

"Didn't you think that about your mother? How long has she been wandering around the prairies now?"

"That's different."

"How? The Committee moves people around like pawns. If they said 'go', you'd be gone."

"So you are saying that we are doomed."

"No, just that we shouldn't assume that everything is going to stay the same."

"The Committee has given me a new assignment."

"You didn't think it relevant to tell me?"

"It was just a couple of days ago, and I'm not going anywhere. Well, I am coming here."

The square opens up in front of them, eerily serene in the evening light. Muffled noise makes its way past city hall, only serving to accentuate the silence.

"I've heard of this place," George says. "Never had a chance to come here, though."

"It's strange, being so close to it yet . . ."

The two wander through the space in silence, Natalie giving him the time to become more familiar with it before continuing.

"The first time I came here since I was a kid was six months ago; I was supposed to show a new member of the Committee around."

"They trusted you with that? Do they not know who you are?"

"It was a setup."

"What did he want?"

"'He'?"

"She?"

"'He.' Indoctrination, be part of the solution, that sort of thing."

"And?"

"I am who I am."

"Why here?"

"Old workers' utopia. He was also living here at the time. That's not the point of coming here, though."

"Wait, he might still be living here?" George asks in a whisper. "With the square's acoustics, he could hear every word we've been saying? What the hell?"

"Eh. We're not saying anything questionable."

"Indoctrination? You know that they are just looking for an excuse to take away my guild membership. Look, okay, let's just go to the edge of the square and talk quietly, yes?"

"Fine."

When they reach the edge, Natalie pulls out her flask and takes a drink. She offers it to George, who shakes his head. She shrugs, takes another sip and puts it away.

"This is an interesting place," George says. "I didn't think that we were capable of keeping anything so clean."

"It's clean because it's dead."

"Sure, makes sense. I imagine that this was supposed to be the great gathering space for the people, the center of communal life, and, judging by the noise coming from the other side of the city hall, it didn't quite work out as planned."

"When I met with the guy, he said something odd; that he didn't know the Towers. He didn't say it in the sense of being from out of town and not being familiar with the neighborhood; it was more fundamental, like he was too detached from its creation to ever fully grasp it. As soon as he said it, I thought of Hiroshima."

"Of course. 'You don't know Hiroshima.' It's a classic."

"Then, six months later, I am back here, working with—really, getting in the way of—people tracking down the source of a freakish typhoid outbreak, and Hiroshima came back to me. It's hard to see now, without the sun beating down, but you could imagine the intense heat and light, the lack of life, as being like the bomb. And the dark outlines of the tourists that mill around during the day as mere shadows imprinted on the walls where people used to be. It's dead."

"I guess. Don't you think that minimizes the incomprehensible enormity of the bomb, of people's actions during a war? Wasn't the idea that the French actress had learned all sorts of details about the effects of the bomb, but that no amount of learning after the fact would add up to really understanding the city?"

"An actual, real-life workers utopia is just as incomprehensible, though. It's less tragic than war, of course. Not tragic at all, really. The typhoid outbreak could have happened anywhere, as far as they know. But the aesthetic similarities are just so obvious."

"Perhaps more so in the middle of the day."

"Right."

After a moment of silence, George puts his arms around Natalie's shoulders and whispers into her ear, "You saw nothing of Hiroshima. Nothing."

Natalie does not react.

"You are supposed to say, 'I saw everything. Everything.'" George continues, lightly kissing her neck, her hair, her ear.

Natalie tenses but stays silent.

In a higher pitched voice, George adds, "Like the hospital, I saw it. I'm sure of it. The hospital exists in Hiroshima. How could I have been able to avoid seeing it?"

In his normal pitch: "You did not see the hospital in Hiroshima. You saw nothing of Hiroshima."

"Can you picture them, the two lovers in bed, anonymous at the start? The camera focusing on their bodies, their heads beyond the frame?"

Natalie shrugs him off, takes a step into the square. He tries to gently bring her back, without insistence. She pulls further away. He follows and they find themselves once more out in the open.

"I'm sorry," he says, just loud enough for her to hear him. "I thought that that's why you brought me here; you figured that I would appreciate the reference to the film. I do appreciate it, by the way."

"Let's just go."

"Wait, really?"

Natalie starts walking toward the closest metro station, on the other side of city hall.

"Let's at least get something to eat before we go," George suggests.

Natalie hesitates, then nods.

"The funny thing about the town where I am filming is that, for exterior shots, we can't point north. At the north end of the valley, there is a cluster of factories surrounded by a wasteland. Absolutely nothing grows there. As you go farther out, there are some plants, stunted trees. By the time you hit the village, everything is green and normal. The original plan was to record the harmony between the traditional way of life and new industry, but with the no man's land like a giant chasm between the two, we couldn't make it work. So, the focus shifted to traditional visuals.

"We encourage people to talk about their work. They are all so happy to be able to stay in the village, to have jobs. They are really proud of what they are doing, refining the metals and mixing the alloys of the future. Almost as proud as they are of their gardens. The ones that don't have any visible health problems, we show on screen. The others, we use as voiceovers for tight shots of liquid zinc or life at the south end of the valley. We've gone through caseloads of lozenges; some people just can't stop coughing. In a couple of cases, we just wrote down what they said and one of the crew repeated it. The crew is pretty small though, and none of us are very good at changing our voices."

"You never talk about work," Natalie points out.

"Yeah, well, we needed a change of subject. I couldn't think of anything else."

"You care too much."

"Probably."

"Did you ask them about the dead zone?"

George shrugs. "I shouldn't have brought all that up."

"Why?"

"It's depressing. It'll spoil the evening."

"This is a perfect evening for spoiling. You might as well let it all out now. Kebab?"

"Yeah, sure. For the kebab, I mean."

They head to a garishly lit fast food joint across the street and half a block away from the Caskets. George is mesmerized by the black light emanating from the cabaret, painting the countless white surfaces in every direction an eerie violet.

"What's that place?" George asks.

"The Cabaret of the Three Caskets. Yes, it's an odd name. Legend has it that Death frequented the place in the old days."

The kebab joint is half empty. A large television near the back is tuned to a Turkish station, the volume high enough to make conversation difficult. They eat quickly and in silence, before finding themselves once more in the street.

"I just feel like such a selfish bastard, is all," George blurts out, staring at the cabaret. "I mean, I should care about the fact that all these people are bringing death home with them from the factories. It stares me in the face every time I look at a clip of one of them. I should care about my integrity as a filmmaker. I should be pointing the camera north, including the diseased faces, the stories cut short by coughing fits. I should shake these people awake. What the hell is wrong with me?"

"You are speaking too loud, first of all."

George moves to the edge of the street, away from passers-by, and continues in a more moderate tone.

"It would almost be better if I was one of them. They look in the mirror and are completely blind to the fact that their job is killing them. They are so proud; they pity me for having to live in the city. At least what they make is real, solid. All I do is film fantasies that nobody believes."

"Would you prefer that people believed them?"

"No. Well, yes. I really do, and I am a selfish bastard for it. No matter how stupid it is, I can't help thinking that the skepticism is a reflection on me. I am not talented enough to put together a story sufficiently engrossing for the audience to get lost in it. I am just waiting for some random bureaucrat to tear up my guild membership, saying that I am hindering the efforts to create a record of real people. Hell, he would probably ask me to tear up my own card, and I would do it."

"No, you wouldn't."

"Yeah, that would take principle or strength of will or, I don't know."

The conversation pauses as a couple walks by, passing within a couple of feet.

"Why do they want films of idyllic villages, anyway?" Natalie asks, once they have more space.

"They don't, at least not in isolation. They want the connection to industry. That's the central point. But industry that is not surrounded by a circle of death. They don't want a chronicle of how the workers bring death home with them, how they contaminate their homes and families."

George points toward the cabaret. "If they have to have death, it needs to be romanticized like the cabaret or the square; an epic myth intensely human yet too large to affect daily life. Something that puts into relief the grand movements of history.

"Ah, who am I kidding? Twenty or thirty years ago, that would have been the case. Back when your father was able to write. Now, death only in moderate doses. I actually like that. I could recut the film to show the slow decline of the workers as the heavy metal poisoning sets in."

"You should do it."

"I should forget about it. We should be at your place, doing what we do moderately well. Not only would it give us more pleasure than standing on a street corner, we will live up to the lofty, weighty goals of our time. Embrace mediocrity, the surest route to happiness!"

"You know how to turn a girl on."

"There is a non-negligible chance that I will fall asleep as soon as we get comfortable. I don't want to get your hopes up. And, besides, you are the one who walked away earlier. You lost your claim on extraordinary."

"Emulating a messed-up French actress still haunted by the death of her German lover at the end of the war? I guess that would have been extraordinary, but not in the way you are imagining."

"You are just focusing on the wrong parts."

"Are we leaving, then?"

"One drink first, and not from your flask."

"It's almost empty, anyway."

Without considering if there were other options close by, the two walk through the halo of black light into the cabaret. A haze of smoke and an off-kilter melody of a synthesizer greet them at the door, followed by a surly looking bouncer with an American-style moustache. He stares at Natalie, clearly hesitating between letting them in or not. Natalie stares back with a veneer of hostility over her general indifference.

"She's old enough," George says. "Ask for her papers if you think she looks too young."

"Too young?" the man responds in disbelief. "What an idea. She looks wasted, or like she forgot to take her medication. She looks like a stray that's going to take a shit in the middle of the living room. And I'm the one who's going to have to clean it up."

"Well, 'she' thinks that, with such a penetrating gaze and profound wisdom, you should have already made a decision and stopped wasting 'her' time," Natalie intones.

"I would have told you that you weren't getting in if it wasn't for him." The bouncer points back to the barely visible stage, where a wraith-like singer begins to feed his microphone a monotone poetry. The words float over the crowd, buoyed by the energy of the synthesizer. After a handful of measures, the two voices are joined by a guitar that matches the singer, adding insistence to the words.

"By all rights, the lyrics should be drowned out," George comments.

"If a guy that looks like he just came out of a concentration camp is on stage, who am I to say that the sickly and infirm don't belong in the audience?" the bouncer asks.

"Sickly and infirm?" Natalie asks.

"Yeah, people like you."

Natalie laughs, and then suddenly becomes serious. "Yes, exactly like me. Are you going to stop wasting our time?"

He reflects a moment longer, before shaking his head and motioning for them to go in.

"What is wrong with young people," he mutters to himself. "They can't even appreciate how good we have it now."

The words are lost on Natalie and George, who are sucked into the ambiance. Nothing feels quite right, but in a comforting way. The band barely holds together, the notes only landing close to the beat. The movement of the crowd follows this approximation faithfully, putting itself constantly out of balance. The violet light of the street warms to steady pink inside. The energy of the music crashes—or, more accurately, stumbles—into it without effect.

George, mesmerized by the scene, stands at the edge of the crowd. Natalie goes to the bar and orders two beers and a shot. She downs the shot before rejoining George with the beers.

"Thanks," George says distractedly. "Why aren't they in jail?"

"Maybe the singer went on a hunger strike, so they released them."

"How can they be playing?"

"The police, like everyone else, rarely leave the capital proper. Maybe with Andesmas on the Committee, that will change. This place will become the mecca he seems to think it is; a workers' paradise on earth."

"Andesmas?" George asks, only half listening.

"The guy I showed around."

"The lyrics are tortured."

"Hmmm? Yeah, I guess they are. For synth-pop, at any rate."

"How can they be playing?"

"You already asked that."

"They are just doing it, without overthinking anything."

"You don't know that."

"I would freeze up at the thought of . . ."

George lapses into silence as the singer's voice becomes more forceful, taking flight from the uneven soundscape of the instruments. The sharp edges of the words, carried by the unrelenting frequency, start to work their way through the monotony and cut into the crowd.

". . . of just expressing something. Honestly expressing something. No editing. Goddamn it, I can't even enjoy this without obsessing about work. Tonight is not a great night for me."

He drains his beer before continuing.

"You're okay if we leave?"

Natalie follows his example. When her glass is empty, she takes his and brings both back to the bar. Then they walk out the door into the cool purple street.

Natalie turns to the bouncer, who is staring off into space.

"You are going to miss an opportunity to call me a mangy stray again . . ."

"Call you a what, now?"

"But, shockingly enough, I am house trained."

"So long as you're walking away, you're none of my concern."

"To think that I am coming back to the cabaret in the morning," Natalie says to George, once they have left the halo and the walls around them are once more a stark white.

"Really?"

"It's more of a café in the morning. The public health inspector seems to be using it as his headquarters, at least while he figures out the typhoid thing."

"Typhoid."

"Yeah. I mentioned it earlier."

"You are doing something good."

"More getting in his way."

"But you aren't trying to cover it up."

"It's not important enough to rate a cover-up. All the Committee is concerned about is seafood imports."

The conversation ends as Natalie and George descend into the metro's tunnels and are no longer able to distance themselves from other people.

Chapter 5

Natalie sits at the table at the Caskets, absentmindedly gazing at the stained-glass window and swishing the lemon teabag around the cup. The regular stream of amoebas, with the occasional ox, ordering coffee offers a continuous, mechanical movement with a steadier rhythm than the band the evening before. The daily routine is followed without a trace of discord or rebellion. Natalie wonders idly if there is any overlap between the morning and evening crowds.

The evening had ended relatively early, with George going back to his place as soon as they exited the metro. He apologized for being so grumpy, thanked Natalie for showing him the neighborhood and then was off. Natalie wandered back to her apartment through the hodgepodge of buildings whose colors were dulled by the streetlights. When she arrived, she sat at her kitchen table with her empty flask directly in front of her, surrounded by several reference books on typhoid fever. She stared at it intently, as if she was having an intense debate. After half an hour, she sighed, got up and put it in a cupboard, out of sight. Then she got ready for bed, avoiding as much as possible looking at herself in the mirror.

This morning did not lend itself to thought. She put on her insipid amoeba uniform with the same sort of automation as the parade of coffee drinkers she would see later. She was halfway to the office before she realized that she wasn't supposed to be going there. The potential repercussions of how late she was going to be by the time she reached the cabaret did not cross her mind, nor hurry her step. When she did finally arrive, the fact that André was not there was noted without any speculation as to why. She simply ordered her tea and sat down at the table he occupied the day before.

The question regarding the overlapping crowds is the first sign that her brain is starting to warm up. The evening scene in the cabaret was strange. It was not so much that a band clearly not advancing the common project, as Andesmas was fond of saying, was playing, but rather the lack of police presence. Typically, there would be three black cars across the street from any event of questionable morals. The police would note the people's presence, which would then be added to files like those Natalie has been looking over in the office. The music would have been considered subversive, so listening to it was illegal. Instead of shutting it down, the police, or the Committee, would use people's presence there at their convenience to encourage certain actions, like signing the counter-charter, or removing annoyances from society for a while. The three black cars were a not-so-subtle hint that the place was to be avoided if one didn't want to risk the consequences.

Neither Natalie nor George care much about their files. For Natalie, it is mainly a reaction to her parents' overprotection in keeping her and her sister away from anything remotely illicit. Their motives were noble, to ensure that the girls would not be condemned to a miserable life as a result of youthful indiscretions. The problem was that tiptoeing around anything that might be offensive to the central authorities was itself a recipe for a miserable—or, more accurately, unlived—life. When the ultimate goal of the government was, in the name of maintaining order, to make it so everyone was guilty of something, trying to avoid it was a fool's game. This fact was confirmed when she was assigned to look through files at work.

This was one of the many practices that the original charter denounced. It went against the constitution and several international agreements that the government had signed. The point of the charter was to remind the Committee of its obligations toward citizens and, on a certain level, all people. Natalie only learned after the fact that her parents had signed it. Her father might have even written portions of it; she doesn't know but wouldn't be surprised. In one symbolic gesture, they threw away years of careful planning and decisions. They finally realized that it was all futile. The day after the dissemination, the three black cars and all the other symbols of the regime were still there. A couple of the leaders went to prison, but most, including her parents, were punished by the simple fact that they had to go on living their lives in a world indifferent to their efforts, surrounded by people unmoved by the call to fight against systemic injustice.

Their impetuous act changed the course of Natalie's existence by barring her from higher education. This was another tactic denounced in the charter; ransoming the future of the children to ensure the obedience of the parents. Honestly, Natalie has no idea whether that really changed all that much, since it would have been unlikely that she would have thrived at university. She would have shot off her mouth, offended someone, stepped on everyone's toes and have ended up in some re-education camp, followed by who knows what sort of random job they would have stuck her with.

Suffice to say that it was strange that there were no black cars last night. It was as if the Towers was some alternate world. It was perhaps stuck in time; perhaps in the moment paradise was realized. It stayed just as clean and pure as in the beginning, immediately after the cataclysmic event. It is only when looking in the corners that one notices the yellow-grey tinges that betray a lack of perfection. It is haunted by anachronistic diseases and superstitions, and subject to freak events that escape such mundane burdens as standard state surveillance.

There is no way to know whether the morning and evening crowds are the same. Everyone now fits into the continuum between plodding ox and insipid amoeba. There are touches of individuality here and there, but nothing that obviously connects to yesterday's pink, synthetic atmosphere. It would be unseemly and needlessly provocative to deviate from the ordinary uniform during the day. The city is, however, still an alternate world in the daytime. It is still the workers' paradise of old that inspired Andesmas's drive toward progress. Provocation does not make sense without the usual norms of society in place. Natalie can only conclude that she is far from knowing exactly how insulated this place is from the rest of society.

A moment later, a couple of minutes before nine o'clock, André and Helen enter the cabaret. They are friendly and animated, as if in the middle of recounting an amusing shared experience. When they see Natalie, the humor dissipates, leaving sober faces weighed down by decades of experience. André comes to the table with a file box while Helen goes to the counter.

"The medical files for the survivors," André states.

"Good. We can get to work. I'm good with files, better than rummaging through people's homes at any rate."

"You can't look at the files."

"What?"

"They are confidential. Only medical staff directly linked to the individual in question are authorized to see them."

"That doesn't make any sense. All that information is included in the central files. All I have been doing for the past six months is going through central files."

André does not respond. Natalie knows that what she said was nonsensical; the rules of the central office are very different than those other members of society must follow. In the middle of the silence, Helen comes to the table with two coffees. Once she has settled in, she takes a form thick with carbon copies out of her satchel, lays it on the table and pulls the box toward her. She goes through all the files and checks them against the form. When she is satisfied that all the files are recorded, she passes it to André. He signs without paying much attention and slides it back to her. She pulls out a pink copy and hands it back.

"The files are now your responsibility," Helen says to André, clearly for the benefit of Natalie.

Helen quickly drinks her coffee and then gets up to leave. She nods to Natalie, seeming to be on the verge of telling her something. She changes her mind and leaves, patting André on his shoulder in passing.

"Okay, so what can I do?" Natalie asks André.

André shrugs as he pulls the box back in front of him.

"It's a pretty public place for confidential files."

"People here do not get involved in what does not concern them."

"True enough, but still. A page could go astray."

"People in government offices are more curious."

"Right. Like me. I get it."

"I wasn't thinking of you."

"Huh. Anyway, regardless, I have a suggestion. Basically, we are looking for a vector common to everyone who got sick. I will do up a chart of all common vectors for diseases spread by fecal matter. As you go through the files, tell me anytime one seems probable and I will write it down. Then we will have the results in a handy, easily readable sheet. I will just label the files as one through however many you have, so you don't have to worry about me knowing who we are talking about. Sound good?"

"How long will it take you to draw up the chart?"

"Oh, it's already done." Natalie pulls a folded piece of paper out of her bag and spreads it out, facing André.

"This is quite thorough."

"Yeah. As much as I'd like to take credit for it, I just copied it from one of the books I flipped through yesterday afternoon."

"You learned about the disease? You didn't have to."

"What can I say? I was curious. Exactly what you feared."

"That is not the sort of curiosity I am concerned about."

"So, are we using the chart?"

"Yes." André opens the box and takes out the first file. "File one."

André goes through the file with a painstaking attention to detail, which makes Natalie doubt that her idea was a good one. Perhaps she should have suggested that she leave and do something else while André does his work. She could have justified it by saying that he would be able to concentrate better without worrying about whether someone so curious might sneak a peek. What will he do if he has to go to the washroom? That goes too far; even if she wasn't here, he couldn't just leave the files on the table. Still, it will be worse knowing that she is here.

"Sewage," André says, without looking up.

Natalie checks the box. She looks back at the thinning coffee line.

"Why are people here dressed in the uniform of the capital?" she wonders out loud.

"A lot of people work in the capital."

"Ah. There are no jobs here, then."

"Food."

Natalie checks the box.

"That is probably why the Towers is considered a failed workers' paradise," Natalie continues her train of thought. "In a lot of ways, it seems to be thriving, in its own way. Perhaps not enough to be considered a paradise, but not so little as to be labeled a failure, either. I mean, it has its warts, but a paradise doesn't have to be perfect."

André continues to flip through the pages of the file and does not respond.

"Maybe 'paradise' is too relative. Affordable housing with indoor plumbing was probably considered a miracle in the beginning. Then, it was just standard, expected. How can a utopia survive the drudgery of everyday life?"

André finishes with the first file, pulls out the second. "File two."

Natalie makes the note. She suddenly wishes that Andesmas would show up. In retrospect, it's surprising that he hadn't already come and gone, assuming of course that he still lives there. Maybe his idealism was quickly crushed by the other members of the Committee and he had taken up residence in the exclusive enclave close to the center of power. Maybe he had actually come through but she hadn't noticed him, since everyone looked the same. That would support her supposition that he had worn a special, light conducting suit for their meeting. Maybe he had never lived in the Towers; it was all part of the ruse to bring her closer into the fold. Maybe he was an actor all along, simply there to feel her out. It's not as if she had the faces and names of the political upper crust memorized.

Whatever the case is, at least he wasn't dull. André probably isn't dull either; it is just the effect of the ox costume. In Andesmas's light suit, he would probably be more animated than he was with Helen when they entered the cabaret. Even if the whole Andesmas episode was fake, there is something to be said for energy and idealism. If the Towers has anything still going for it, it was an overabundance of both.

"Water," André says.

"Indoor plumbing, fountain or standing?"

"Indoor plumbing."

It is the people that are all wrong. Everyone who has come through the cabaret this morning would feel right at home in her office. She pictures herself in her office, filled with neutral colors and the steady hum of paper and hushed voices. She would be looking through the red files, looking for ways to bring the people they represent to the insipid normal or promote them as a convenient, temporary figurehead. Files are undoubtedly piling up on her desk as she sits here playing disease vector bingo. Maybe the quota of signatures would be reached before she gets back, and she will be able to move on to other tasks. She feels that she is only kidding herself; even with the counter-charter done, there will always be reasons to move people around the board.

She instinctively reaches into the pocket where she usually keeps her flask. Finding the pocket empty, she remembers last night and her foolish decision to put it in the cupboard, out of sight. She contemplates ordering something stronger than her lemon tea, but quickly dismisses it. If only boredom would slow down her thoughts and dull their sharp edges, rather than providing them with a playground filled only with equipment that turns, spins, repeats endlessly. The thoughts don't even have the decency to get dizzy, the millionth time they circle around. To top it all off, she can't recall the train of thought that led to the decision.

André continues, somehow making turning pages into a plodding movement. The chart slowly fills, without any pattern that Natalie can discern. She swirls her teabag in the now empty cup until the string pulls loose from the bag.

"Water," she says.

"What?" André replies. "No, the last one was solid refuse."

"The file of the guy who oversaw the capital's water treatment facility crossed my desk a couple of months ago. Quite the character."

"Hervé Marne?"

"The same. Do you know him?"

"We've crossed paths."

"Makes sense. He was a real war hero, apparently."

"In a matter of speaking."

"Yeah, I suppose it wasn't in the traditional sense."

"Right."

"He saved a lot of lives, though. Sure, it was just chlorinating water for the troops. But really, how many soldiers on the front die of disease?"

"I don't know."

"I bet it was a huge number, stuck in trenches for months on end. Sure, they probably died later anyway in the fighting. At least they would have been doing what they were there to do, whatever one thinks of the war. To get there and die of some random disease just because the water wasn't clean seems even worse."

"He didn't save them."

"Right, like I said."

"No, that's not what I meant. The troops didn't drink the water. They couldn't stand the smell and taste of the chlorine. Too much was used, much more than is the norm today. The soldiers typically drank dirty water out of shell craters or whatever else they could get their hands on. What saved them was vaccination, which the army made mandatory well before the war. Some still died—the vaccines used were not one hundred percent effective— but most made it through. To die later, as you said."

"That is the most I have ever heard you say at one time. I'm shocked."

André shrugs and turns another page.

"So, what you are saying is that Marne is a fraud?"

"He got it right later. The capital's system, which covers the region, works well enough."

"'Well enough'?"

"Food."

Natalie checks the box. "I am just surprised that the early failure didn't make it into the file. Or, perhaps it did. It was a while ago. But I think I would have remembered."

"You trust the files?"

"Yes. Well, I haven't thought about it much. It's not as if I can compare them to the real thing, so it's always seemed beside the point. I prefer not thinking about the actual people, to be honest. They are very detailed, though. I don't imagine that it is that much different than trusting these medical files."

"I know who prepared these files and they were written up after direct contact with the subjects."

"Right, but central files are just meta-files. They are a compilation of files like these. Analyses might be added, but they are labelled as such."

André does not respond.

"I guess I wouldn't know if someone altered something. They would have to do a thorough job of it, and it's hard to imagine why anyone would go through the effort. The direct files overlap a great deal, so they would all have to be changed to keep everything consistent."

Natalie starts twisting the string around her finger, untwisting it, then twisting it again. André continues to turn pages.

"Besides that, everyone is guilty, so what's the point?" She then circles around to "What do you mean by 'well enough'?"

"It works. It could work better. The water doesn't make people sick. That is what matters."

"Can you say that before you figure out the source of the fever?"

André nods. "The water from the plant is tested. After it leaves the plant, we don't know."

Chapter 6

"You know," George says, "there are no rules against you wearing a bit of color to work."

Natalie looks back toward the bed after buttoning up her blouse. "Yes, but there is a rule against you making comments like that when you stay over."

"Nobody will notice anyway. They are too busy minding their own business. You can do it for yourself."

"With the number of people who have commented lately that I look like death warmed over, I would say that I attract far too much attention already."

"Maybe some color will balance that out."

"Maybe you should take a page out of nobody's book."

"Right, well have fun tracking down your disease."

George turns over and goes back to sleep. Natalie shakes her head and goes into the kitchen, where her already refilled flask is waiting for her in the middle of the table.

"You don't give me stupid recommendations, do you?" she asks the flask softly before slipping it into her pocket.

She is meeting Andesmas's amoeba, whose name escapes her, at her office before going to the Towers. She hopes that the brief words André suggested suffice, as she has nothing else to say.

"It is absolutely not seafood, unless there was a batch soaked in human excrement that made its way through inspections," she opens when she is once more in the small meeting room with the prize specimen of insipid amoebas.

"Fine, good. We believed that already—except the excrement part—but it is good to have that confirmed. Do you know the source?"

"No, not yet. It's only been a couple of days."

"This is a Committee priority."

"That's nice. Must be why they put me on it, what with all my education and experience in public health."

"Your role is as a liaison, not as a health professional."

"Yeah, I got that. Is that all?"

"Your attitude has been noticed, you know."

"And?"

"And there will be repercussions, sooner or later."

Natalie counts to ten. "Sure. Is that all?"

"Let me know when you have a probable source. We don't have time to wait until Mr. Monnier is completely sure."

Natalie nods, gets up and leaves. Fifteen minutes later, she is walking from the metro station to the cabaret. She notices André outside, looking at the partially cloudy sky. She slows her pace to see how long he stays like that when no one is around. He takes his time, scanning the sky as if reading lines on a page. Then he slowly lowers his gaze. When he sees Natalie, he starts walking toward her. He breaks his stride a moment later as he passes a group of kids, but does not stop.

"What did you see?" Natalie asks.

"I think that one of those kids is Theo."

"How can you tell?"

"The apartment was filled with pictures of the kids."

"Ah. I didn't notice."

André looks at her incredulously.

"What can I say? I am not very observant. Which one is he?"

"Slender, blond, red shirt."

"What's on the official agenda?"

"Another interview and inspection. Adult siblings, the sister died."

André glances regularly back at the kids. When they start moving, he turns, then thinks better of it and turns back.

"We are supposed to be there at nine thirty."

"'We'? I'll just get in the way. Why don't I follow Theo?"

"That's not a good idea."

"I won't talk to him or anything. I'll just see where he goes so we have an easier time finding him later."

André hesitates, then nods.

The group is almost out of sight, so Natalie wastes no time in following them. The street is filled with a light morning crowd that flows around the myriad random vehicles parked on the sidewalk. The vehicles are used as glorified delivery trucks and will magically disappear in an hour or two. Natalie hasn't really paid attention to them before, mainly due to how common they are in the capital and to the fact that she can see over most of them. Only now that she is trying to follow a child do they seem like obstructions.

Luckily, the red shirt is neither common nor subtle, so she is able to catch regular glimpses of it heading up the street toward the square. Before it reaches the ground zero of the city, it suddenly veers to the side and disappears. When Natalie arrives at more or less the spot where Theo disappeared, she looks down the side street and through the front windows of the stores on either side. There is no patch of red in sight. Judging that the side street was his most likely route, she leaves the main stream of people and vehicles behind and finds herself in a space of pure white. There are no windows, no doors, no details on either side of the route. The only color comes from a crew of painters in a variety of muted browns and greys finishing up covering over graffiti in shades of green. She slows her stride once again, this time to watch the last color on the wall disappear. She is tempted to share her thoughts on the effect the emaciated trees in the square have in emphasizing the austere whiteness of the space.

"Wouldn't it be better to leave a hint of color, in order to bring out just how white the rest of the space is?" she asks as she passes the crew.

"It depends on whether you want the color to complement the architectural forms or just use the wall as a blank canvas," one of the painters replies.

Natalie stops short, not really having viewed the painters as complete people capable or inclined to respond to her idea.

"What's the difference?" she asks.

"The graffiti was placed for convenience. It deserves a frame to pull it out from the background of the wall."

The painter takes a small brush and a can of paint from the pile of material, gives the can a quick, vigorous shake, pops the lid, dips the brush and sketches a dark grey frame around nothing. Then she grabs another can, goes through the ritual and recreates the last bit of graffiti in the bottom left one third of the frame. The whole crew looks at Natalie, who is staring at the wall. Then they dip their rollers and cover the scene with white paint and continue along their way.

Natalie stares at the white wall as the crew moves on. It is, if anything, more purely white than the square but lacking in the energy that would make Andesmas shine and the space resemble—at least for her—Hiroshima. On the other hand, it seems even more like the movie, with the film crew of the movie within the movie always just glimpsed as it moves on after a scene. Then she has a moment of panic; the red shirt is probably long gone, assuming that Theo even took this path. She decides that it is not really that important. Looking at the painting that existed a moment ago, she slowly concludes that it did not relate to the architecture. It remains a mystery whether that is better or worse for accentuating the whiteness. She then slowly walks away, to the first intersection where myriad choices await.

Since Theo is probably far away, or back in one of the stores she passed, Natalie turns into the most interesting street. Above her head on both sides are massive stained-glass windows in abstract patterns. They are dull in the middle of the overcast day, resembling ersatz details painted on the wall more than real windows. She looks up to see smaller windows regularly placed all the way up to the top of the towers. They are undoubtedly hallway windows, like the one she saw from the inside the other day. As she continues forward, she trips on a break in the pavement. She stops her fall with a hand on the wall, before hastily removing her hand, worried momentarily that a yellow-grey handprint would be left behind.

She focuses her attention on the pavement, which seems to be ordinary grey asphalt. After looking closer, she realizes that it too is painted. Its length is buckled and uneven, probably patched to reduce the peaks and valleys as much as possible without tearing the whole thing up and repaving it. The paint creates the visual illusion that it is flatter and more consistent than it really is. She wonders if the walls aren't really as smooth as they seem, if there are cracks running through all these utopian buildings. A touch of discoloration seems like a minor thing in relation to the structures slowly crumbling, but she can't bring herself to run her hand along the wall to confirm her suspicions. In any case, it seems to her that the real part of the realized utopia is, over time, pulling away from the ideal, no matter how many layers of paint are added.

The windows, already somewhat less interesting than they would be if light were shining through them, lose their attraction. Natalie speeds up and focuses more on not stumbling than anything else. She almost wishes that the wall she had leaned on had been rougher; that she had scratched her hand on it and left some blood there. It wouldn't have had much of an impact without a complementary frame but would have made the space seem less anonymous. It might have also tempted fate, although she imagines that Death would be more sophisticated than a shark; blood in the water for her would be the smell of fresh pestilence at the outset of an epidemic.

Natalie turns another corner and finds herself in front of a row of local shops. The incongruous signs and awnings make it clear that ideals and utopias were the furthest things from the shopkeepers' minds when they set up here. She is once again in the midst of a flow of people, even if she would characterize it as a mere trickle. Although she could easily wend her way around them, she decides to match their unhurried yet purposeful pace.

For some reason, she had held out hope that the influence of the capital—and the world—would be less here, away from the main drag, but people look, if not exactly grey, at least as faded as anywhere else. They fit better in this motley commercial microcosm and in the yellow-grey pseudo-whiteness of their homes than in the immaculate white of the square or surrounded by the vibrant colors of the stained glass—at least when there is enough light to give the glass life. The city will have to invest in crews of roving tailors and barbers who can give people a touch-up as needed, as the painters do for the walls.

She turns at the next intersection, mostly because she has taken to not going straight ahead for very long. The street is mainly white, with only the small hallway-style windows and detailing— barely visible without the shadows of a sunny day—that appear to be an attempt to make the buildings look slightly less monolithic. She wonders if she has it wrong; the people need to be considered like the grey painted pavement rather than the white walls. Andesmas was looking for a less flashy sort of Towers, undoubtedly where harmony would reign as everyone worked at advancing the common project. Grey would be the better shade to give a sense of that commonality, while doing away with the constant need for touch-ups and corrections.

Natalie notices that her feet are suddenly cold and wet. She curses her chronic inattention and steps out of a puddle in a depression in the pavement. A faucet, camouflaged in white, sticks out of the wall above it. She notices a drain a couple of feet away that likely served its purpose well once upon a time. Had she been keeping a list of ways the Towers was no longer a utopia, she would add this.

She looks down the street to get a better sense of her surroundings before her mind starts wandering again. About two blocks away she sees a variety of colors, as if someone had piled all the clothes too bright for respectable people to wear in a lost corner, hidden from sight. She figures that, with her penchant for turning at every intersection, she is only a block off the main street, but she doubts that there is a direct connection between the two spots. One of the more common colors of the pile being red, she once more feels some hope that Theo is not far off. Although it seems too large, the pile could be a group of kids. Once her thoughts have run their course, she decides to actually move and find out what it really is.

As she approaches, she first notes that a child who could be Theo is indeed there. All she has to go off is André's description and several fleeting glimpses of a kid André wasn't entirely sure was Theo, so she has to satisfy herself with suppositions. She takes in the entire scene. At the center is a miniature, multicolored stage where two marionettes are chasing each other with comically over-sized blunt objects. Somehow, the objects are designed to fail in different ways when they make contact; sticks break in half, pipes bend, the mesh in racquets snaps or stretches to resemble butter-fly nets, and so forth. In front sits a small group of children of various ages. Some are already dressed in the grey uniforms of their parents, assuming that they have parents. As far as Natalie knows, they could pretty much all be orphaned street urchins, fallen through the cracks of Andesmas's vaunted common project. It is not as if the Committee can prioritize everything, and inter-national seafood agreements are far more visible and troublesome than easily distracted miniature people. Most are wearing clothes with splashes of color, which does not necessarily contradict the street urchin theory.

The boy she takes to be Theo is near the back, one of the older kids in the group. He doesn't seem to be taken in by the violent antics in front of him. Natalie imagines that he is watching it more out of nostalgia than enjoyment. His little brother probably used to be just as mesmerized as the younger kids in the front. It then occurs to Natalie that nobody is laughing; there is just a feeling in the air of unhinged amusement, of playful energy at odds with the austere, quasi-apocalyptic surroundings. If it wasn't for the color, the scene could be from an old Buster Keaton movie. The kids are listening to the orchestration playing in their heads.

Not being able to help herself, Natalie leans toward the perhaps Theo and whispers, "Why is no one laughing?"

The boy jolts upright, sizes her up—or at least her insipid amoeba costume—in an instant and yells, "Scatter!"

Before Natalie has a chance to react, the kids disperse in all directions. She weighs whether it is worth chasing them in her still soggy shoes and decides against it. Instead, she sits down in front of the stage, checks her watch and pulls out her flask. At first, she doesn't pay attention to the two puppeteers who have poked their heads up from the stage and are looking at her with curiosity.

After a pause, Natalie says, "Sorry for scaring away your audience."

She focuses on the puppeteers, both young women dressed from head to toe in black, probably about her own age. They look impossibly smooth, unmarked by anxiety or any other of the asperities of life. She can't imagine anyone telling them that they don't look well. She also has trouble seeing how they would fit in to Andesmas's grey utopia. She offers them the flask, and is unsurprised when they refuse politely.

"It happens fairly regularly," one of the women says. "I wouldn't worry about it."

"Shouldn't they be in school?"

"Probably," the second replies. "If they are not going to go, there are worse things for them to be doing in the meantime."

"Watching mindless violence?"

"We were experimenting with materials today," the second says.

"It is a traditional art form, part of our national identity," the first adds. "Normally we recount traditional stories, as well. We can't do that every day though. Regardless, the authorities know that we are here."

"A trap for the kids?"

"They tried that at the beginning, but the kids were too skittish," the second responds. "I'm surprised that you got as close as you did."

"I don't come off as much of a threat," Natalie states. "Are you from the School of Puppetry?"

"We're students there, yes," the first says.

"Students of Tonda Keller?"

"He's one of our profs. Do you know him?"

"In a matter of speaking. He has done some great work in keeping the tradition alive."

"Yes, he has," the second says with some hesitation.

"I was looking for a kid named Theo. I don't suppose you know him?"

"Not really."

"Why?" the first asks.

"I am working with the public health group. His brother, Albert, passed away a short time ago and we are piecing together how he got sick. Theo would be a great help in doing that."

The two puppeteers give each other a shocked look at the name of Albert.

"Albert is gone?" the first asks in disbelief.

Natalie nods.

"He always went to school," the second says. "But afterward . . . I don't think he paid much attention in class. He would come with ideas, all sorts of ideas for new stories. He was fixated on the realm of the Squirrel King. Squirrel King the First, he would always correct people if they just said the Squirrel King. We tried to convince him that his ideas would be more spectacular if he knew about the stories already written. He was too young, didn't have the patience."

"He would still sit quietly and watch the plays," the first interjects.

"We could tell that his mind was elsewhere ten minutes in," the second continues. "He picked up details here and there, without ever managing to grasp how it all hung together."

"Maybe if it was Dr. Keller or another master storyteller, he would have gotten more out of it," the first says.

"Master storytellers don't do street theatre anymore," the second points out. "And could you imagine them coming all the way out here?"

"Well, in any case, it sounds like you know Theo," Natalie says.

"He was here today," the first says. "For the past couple of weeks he has come pretty much every day. I suppose, since his brother got sick . . ."

"Are you going to be here tomorrow?" Natalie asks.

"Yes," the second says, "but it takes about a week for the kids to come back. If you are with the government, why don't you try him at home? You have to know where he lives."

"Because I am with the government, and he only comes home in the evenings."

"Really? There is a disease killing kids around here and you can't work evenings?"

"The outbreak has been handled, although they might have missed you two in the vaccination drive. So, it isn't an emergency. At least that's what I understand, haven't been doing this for very long."

"Vaccination drive?!" the first questions Natalie.

"Right, you are going to be here tomorrow?"

"Yes," the second says, "you already asked."

"In this spot specifically?"

"Yes."

"I'll let the doctor know. Her name is Helen. Very professional, even if her bedside manner could use some work."

"Thank you," the first says.

Natalie shrugs, gets up and makes her way down the street. When she is a certain distance away, she pulls out her flask. She has already had enough of her mind running away with her. She chooses without fail the most direct path back to the cabaret, thankful once more for the unexpected skills picking up dirty laundry when she was younger gave her. As she approaches the door, her control slips and she imagines what life might have been like if she had been able to attend a place like the National School of Puppetry. Despite having no interest in it, she can't help believing that her existence would somehow be better. Then she tells herself to stop whining.

André is at the table, looking over her chart. Natalie orders a lemon tea and joins him. André looks up and says, "It might be the water."

Chapter 7

Natalie scans the street for a blond boy, without any luck. It doesn't matter to her overly much if he turns out to be Theo or not; all she wants is an excuse to skip another house visit, while coming off as at least somewhat professional. Alas, no one sticks out from the crowd.

"Helen asked me to thank you for the information on the street actors," André says.

"Puppeteers," Natalie corrects distractedly, still holding out some hope.

"Yes. We are going to see a more traditional family today. Two parents, husband and wife, and formerly two kids."

The glimmer of hope dies. Natalie does not bother asking for the names or other details. This time, she will not make a mess in the kitchen. She will pay attention to the photos, but avoid everything else. That is the game plan, at least.

The lobby of this building is much more ornate than the last one, with a vast stained-glass window in the back wall. Natalie pauses when she realizes that this is one of the windows she passed yesterday. It appears very different when looking at it directly from an appropriate distance and with light from outside pouring in. Nothing in the space looks white, but she can smell the faint odor of paint. They go directly to the elevator and take it to the sixth floor. The hallway seems identical to the last building, with the same size of window projecting a small square of color on the wall. The dread Natalie felt before is amplified, with her mind building off her experience and creating a series of ever-worse scenarios.

The father lets them in and shows them to the living room. He appears angry, rather than melancholic, though Natalie hardly notices. His wife is already there, with their young daughter on her lap. The mother seems beaten down, as if she has been carrying the weight of existence for the whole family. The daughter shows

61

a mixture of shyness and curiosity, clearly too young to fully comprehend the loss of her sibling. With everyone there, Natalie quickly examines them, as if they were in a photo, before distancing herself. For all intents and purposes, that fulfills the one thing she promised herself that she would do. If she runs into the daughter in the crowd in front of the miniature stage, she will recognize her. Now all she needs to accomplish is to avoid being pulled into the emotional vortex.

André goes through his usual questions, making an effort both to be personable and keep to his script. His aim is for them to see him as someone who cares, all the while keeping the process consistent so he can compare responses later. The husband does all the talking, but glances at his wife after almost every answer for a quick nod. It is as if he is the dummy and she the ventriloquist. Besides the nods, both mother and daughter are still enough to actually be a picture. It is only when André thanks them, just when he is about to ask to see the child's room, that the pattern is broken.

"What do you think it is?" the husband asks.

"It is too early to draw conclusions," André responds. "I will let you know once we have a definitive answer."

"I'll tell you what it is. Our families are falling apart, and the government doesn't give a shit. Without strong families, we've got nothing but crime, disease and poverty."

"Thank you for your input. Please note that I work for the government."

"Everyone works for the government. But, maybe you are in a position to do something. Maybe Stephen's death could lead to change."

"We aim to make sure that an outbreak like this does not happen again."

"Do you know that I have to commute three hours every day to the factory? Three hours! How am I supposed to see my family? How are we supposed to stay healthy?"

"I am not in a position to improve the transportation system."

"This used to be a workers' town. All the factories were a stone's throw away. I could come home for lunch. Now, there's nothing. No jobs here. Everything was moved away by government decree. Did they ask us? No, they did not."

"The factories were moved for health reasons."

"Health, my arse. That's the story they told us. But did they improve the scrubbers? Did they phase out the old coal plant? No, they did not. I have to commute three hours a day, and then spend my days in the same filth. The exact same filth! Next, you're going to tell me that my kids are kept away from it. That's always the next line. Lies! The factories were just replaced by cars, more and more cars, that spew all sorts of crap. And every building in this town burns coal. This whitewashed town; if the painters went on strike for a week, every surface would be as grey as a hippopotamus."

He gestures emphatically toward a stuffed hippopotamus on the floor.

Natalie is, despite herself, drawn in by the rant. Its odd simile pulls her attention to the toy, alone in the middle of a threadbare carpet. She glances about for more toys, finding only an unpainted wooden figure and several white and dark blue balls in the corner. It doesn't seem like much for two kids, though there are probably more toys in other rooms. What strikes her the most, though, is the lack of color. She thinks back to the last apartment, but can't remember anything but the bright scene on the wall. It is just as well that she hadn't paid attention; she felt uncomfortable enough without being surrounded by toys that seemed to have the joy sucked out of them.

"We used to have an incinerator," the husband continues, "just on the other side of the square. One chimney; the smoke was noticeable, it smelled funny sometimes. And you know what? It was far cleaner than the thousand smaller chimneys pumping out soot that replaced it. Demolishing it was theatre, all just because people—the busybodies from the capital—could see it. We are the ones who bear the brunt; our children bear the brunt."

Natalie's eyes move from the toys to the mother and daughter. If anything, the mother's shoulders are more slumped and the daughter is holding her even tighter, but Natalie can't be sure. She suppresses the urge to reach out to the girl and lead her out of her faded apartment, away from her father's anger. The puppet show, barely two blocks away as the crow flies, is short an audience today. It would welcome such a curious, wide-eyed spectator with open, whimsical arms. Natalie knows that she is not the same as the fresh-faced puppeteers; she would more likely scare the girl and raise the mother's suspicions if she tried anything. They had just lost one member of the family and she, a stray cog of the central bureaucracy, would be proposing to take away another one; what a stupid idea.

"You come here after all that? It takes the death of my son to bring you to my door!"

"Would you mind running through his routine in the morning?" André asks calmly.

"Would I? I . . ." The husband falters and looks at his wife for guidance. She avoids his gaze.

"It would be helpful if we start where he slept."

Natalie focuses on the man just as he deflates, the red tinge of his face fading to the sallow color of someone who rarely sees the sky. He suppresses a coughing fit, which Natalie suspects is not so different from those suffered by the subjects of George's film. He then slowly rises, gives the hippopotamus a half-hearted kick and heads to the boy's room, motioning for André to follow him.

"The foreman said he was so sorry for my loss," he continues his rant in a low grumble, though with an occasional spark. "He bent over backward to give me the time I needed to bury my son, to be here today. Where was he when Stephen was alive? Did he let me take time to spend with my son when he was alive? That would have been to betray the country, the effort to create a better life for everyone. Lies! All those nights worked were just to hide the smoke, so we could use the old furnaces that were supposed to be retired. Efficiency! Progress! It was all about making more, producing more. Work cut off from life. What good are you, coming here now? Plastering over a crack in the wall of a building crumbling all around you."

Once the two men are out of sight, the wife pleads quietly, "Please don't put all that in the report. It's just grief. He doesn't know what he is talking about."

"The only details in the report will be those relevant to the typhoid outbreak," Natalie says, having no idea what André will write.

"Thank you."

Natalie nods and starts to fidget with the flask in her pocket. She concentrates on doing as little as possible, figuring that it might sufficiently compensate for paying attention to the rant. It was unavoidable, but that does not mean that she has to think about what was said. She already has enough fodder to turn over in her head for an eternity. She needs something else, though, so she imagines the hippo running with a lumbering gait on its stubby legs around the room. She wonders if there is a place in her schema for hippos; large and plodding, similar to the ox, but more unpredictable and prone to anger. The husband should probably not be categorized as a hippo—his wife is undoubtedly right about the grief of losing a child, paired with a good dose of frustration and guilt, leading to his outburst—but it feels satisfying to have another animal at ready for her analysis of the people around her. Two does, in retrospect, seem awfully limited.

The hippo tires quickly, as is likely normal for a large animal with stubby legs. Natalie's train of thought outpaces it, feeding off the rant. It is as if the room is imbued with the anger, slowly seeping into her mind. She has little control at the best of times and letting her thoughts go seems like a better choice under the circumstances than pulling out her flask or trying to be less awkward in front of the grieving family, so she mentally writes a large red X next to "avoid everything else."

She had thought of the grey utopia, the utopia she imagined Andesmas aiming toward, as the lesser utopia. It was the uneven society that was walked all over and impossible to keep clean. It was the compromise that would bring everyone to some mediocre middle ground, where life was tolerable, but it would be a stretch to consider it a worthy goal. But then, the original workers' paradise that Andesmas vaunted, that he believed was too lofty a goal for the common project, was not the blinding white city at all. Hiroshima only appeared after the microcosm had been dismantled, when industry had been moved far away, when the city became incomprehensible.

Paradise as a city shadowed by industrial smoke, chemicals and soot raining down, covering every surface; does that make any more sense? That sounds more like a paradise for Death than for workers. It sounds like the misery at the end of the nineteenth century, at least the misery described in the countless books Natalie had read that were set in the period. Maybe she is over-imagining the smoke, though. If it wasn't as bad as cars and the coal that heats the apartments, it probably wasn't so bad. Half the misery from the nineteenth century came from poverty anyway. The Towers was obviously built to provide housing, so other services were probably also in the mix. The city could very well have been the best place workers had ever lived; a paradise, relatively speaking.

The Towers seems more like a museum piece now. It is a symbol fixed in time that does not quite represent what it once was. Andesmas pointed to it as a concrete example of social harmony and the ingenuity of the working class. He didn't care about the details; he wouldn't have cared if it had in reality been just as squalid as an industrial slum at the turn of the century. So long as it is brilliant enough now to inspire people to join in the common project, a prop for his rousing speech, nothing else matters. That could be too cynical, though. After all, the city is still full of people who sully the pure white with their yellow-grey lives. She hasn't seen much evidence of the white rubbing off on them, inspiring a higher level of solidarity than elsewhere. Without Andesmas's explanation, the piece is far too abstract for a shared interpretation.

The sound of the two men coming back into the room shakes Natalie from her train of thought. She notices that the daughter is staring at her with curiosity. She is comforted by the lack of fear or hostility in her eyes. The husband seems to have calmed down; it is likely difficult to stay angry when discussing mundane things such as toothpaste and soap. André waits for him to sit down before thanking the entire family for their help. A moment later, André and Natalie are once more in the street.

"Was he right, regarding the pollution?" Natalie asks.

"He wasn't completely wrong."

"Meaning?"

"Domestic heating and transportation are a health problem."

"Moving industry away was more esthetic than practical, then?"

"No. Certain plants can release far more dangerous chemicals."

"But they can be filtered. They should be filtered anyway."

"The system isn't perfect."

"And it is made worse with the incessant push to increase production."

"Probably."

They lapse into silence.

"He missed two things," André explains after a moment. "The most important is catastrophic risk. Plants can explode, chemicals can leak; accidents happen. The second is nuisance. Industry can be loud, can smell, there might be vibration or other effects. There are many good reasons to separate all that from where people live."

"Fair enough. So, the Towers was never a workers' paradise?"

"It wasn't perfect."

Another silence. Before they enter the cabaret, André stops and turns to Natalie.

"What he said about the city, industry and all the rest, none of it is relevant to the investigation."

"Agreed."

They enter and go through the ritual of ordering and sitting at their usual table. André pulls out the chart, spreads it on the table and adds another line. Then he stares at it, trying to suss out any patterns that might be lurking with the additional data point. Natalie stirs her teabag and suppresses the urge to suggest that they really need to do a real statistical analysis. She has little idea of what would actually be involved and doubts that André could just call on someone to do the work. Perhaps if there was still a question of the culpability of the seafood she could have asked the central bureaucracy for support, but that boat has sailed.

Ten minutes later, Helen walks in. She orders and drinks her coffee at the counter, but still stops by the table.

"I stopped by the puppet show," she says to André. "It was pretty sad, nobody was in the audience."

"You didn't stick around?" Natalie asks. "Apparently, they do some high quality classical work."

Helen looks at her for a minute, seeming to have trouble focusing on rather than looking through her.

"Thank you for telling André about them."

"Hey, no problem. I just want to help out, fight the good fight."

Helen blinks, then starts to turn away.

"Of course, it was me who scared off their audience. Something about being an unholy mix of sickly pariah and loose cog that made them run away. I'll probably have a starring role in their nightmares for years to come. I think that means I am moving up in the world. They were a bunch of street urchins anyway, pulled whole cloth from Dickens. Maybe I scared them back to school; a win-win for everyone but those unsavory puppets."

"You are very strange."

"Thank you."

Helen turns to André, says something that Natalie does not

catch, and then leaves.

"So, have we determined the source?"

"No. The possibilities have been sufficiently narrowed, though, so we can start the tests. They will take a week or two."

"No more house visits?"

"No more interviews, though I would still like to talk to Theo."

"You could just wait for him at his house; he still goes home at night. Or get there early enough in the morning."

André shrugs and Natalie lets it drop.

Chapter 8

The red files piled on each desk gives the office more color than Natalie has seen since the synth-pop show at the cabaret. If Death were after people's essences rather than their fermented blood, this would be the place for her to come. Natalie supposed that she could have written the progress report for Andesmas's personal insipid amoeba at the Caskets, but doing it at the office makes her feel less out of the loop. It would be unwise to forget that her time in the Towers is limited. She will be back here soon enough and would prefer not to be caught completely off guard by a reorganization or the malaise she feels every time she walks through the door.

It seems to her that Death would also be far more at home in this brutalist building, even if it would probably survive a nuclear explosion. As Natalie makes her way across the open space to her desk, though, thoughts of Death fade. No matter how striking the red folders are, no matter how much the concrete of the bunker weighs down on the people inside, concepts like Death, paradise, utopia and all the rest seem fantastical and misplaced. This is the realm of the real in a way the Towers could never be, which is probably just as well for the Towers. Natalie wonders how the insipid amoebas lining up for coffee in the cabaret before making their way to the central government complex deal with such a large shift in mindset every day. Perhaps it is no different from those working in industrial areas at the edge of nowhere, especially if they are surrounded by molten ore or coal furnaces or anything else in the orange-red spectrum.

Natalie hesitates before sitting down at her desk, not entirely sure if it's still hers. Last time she was here, she went straight to the small meeting room without thinking about whether someone else had been assigned the desk. She looks at the files lying on top and notices that they have not changed. Not even those in the finished pile have been taken away. Tonda Keller is still on top. With that assurance, she hangs her jacket on the back of the chair and sits down. She finds it odd, however, that Keller is still there. She starts contemplating what sort of problems the counter-charter might have run into before forcing herself to stop and focus on the task at hand.

There is little to put in the report, so it should be quick. She starts by noting that the event is confirmed to be a typhoid fever outbreak and gives some quick details about how the disease is spread. She states that this rules out the seafood as such, unless it was contaminated in an unrelated way. Given the habits of the victims, most of whom had not eaten seafood in the time period, it is safe to rule it out. This leaves environmental considerations, but it is too early in the investigation to determine which ones. The most probable source is the water system, but, again, it is too early to say for sure. She goes on to describe the vaccination and education programs for people in proximity to the outbreak. The programs can be considered a success as no new cases have been reported. She concludes by saying that this situation is no longer an emergency, but that she will continue to monitor the progress of the investigation and keep the Committee informed.

A strange thing happens as she is typing out the report. Someone comes around with a cart, places new files on the incoming pile and takes the finished pile. Natalie instinctively snatches Keller's file from the latter pile before it is taken away. She feels vaguely guilty about what she wrote in it, probably because of her run-in with the two puppeteers the other day. She dismisses the feeling, deciding that it will probably be useful to keep the file on hand for the future. The next thing she knows, she is looking through a file from the incoming pile. It is as if the area around the desk was in stasis when she was gone and then came back to life as soon as some hidden sensor detected her presence. The Towers already seems like a ridiculous daydream; how could an investigation of rotten seafood in a monochromatic city to avoid an international incident be real?

A colleague calls to her, saying that the weekly issues meeting is about to begin. The meeting is an opportunity to go over potential enticements and embarrassments as a group to make sure that everyone is being consistent. Natalie starts saying that she isn't really there, but then stops, shakes her head and goes to the meeting. If there are any organizational announcements, they will be made there, so she might as well be present.

After the meeting, she goes back to her desk and continues to read through the file she has started. When she has finished putting together the plans to potentially ruin another person's life and to protect the Committee from possible complications she feels as drained as she always has. She takes her usual breaks with her flask and, this time, no one disturbs her with another assignment. She only remembers about the typhoid report when she has her jacket on, ready for the second break of the day. She stuffs it in an internal mail envelope, scrawls Andesmas's name on it and puts it on the appropriate pile at the edge of the office on her way out.

At the end of the day, Natalie joins the amorphous group that regularly heads to a bar just outside of the government district after work. It is what she always did when she was at the office on a daily basis, so she has never really differentiated it from the work experience. It would be comforting to believe that, even if she was part of the machine during the day, she was able to leave her insipid amoeba suit at the door and put on whatever was authentic to her. She has no idea what that version of her would look like. Occasionally, in parallel to her morning thoughts of wearing something else to work, she has tried on different conceptions of herself, more often than not borrowed from others. Nothing allowed her to separate herself completely from the grey suit, no identity stood on its own. It made more sense to just accept it, all the while dulling the sentiments that went along with it.

The group goes through several rounds with practiced efficiency. Nobody is there for a pleasant, casual drink to bolster comradery. Conversation is light, consisting mainly of office gossip. No matter how much alcohol is consumed, talk never swerves into actual work, personal lives beyond broad generalities, politics or anything similar. Due to her absence, Natalie has little to add. Nobody would be so imprudent to ask where she has been or what she has been doing. All the same, she feels perfectly at ease in a group where everyone openly drinks however much they need for the reality of their lives and the suspicion of the impact of their work on other people fade into the background. Some have to contend with how much they care, others their apathy; it all ends in the same place. Everyone is just as unhealthy as Natalie, and it wouldn't occur to any of them to comment on it.

After a couple hours, those with families or who live farther away call it a night. Natalie, generally inclined to stay until the bitter end, finds herself leaving with the first wave. The others will continue on, eventually ending at the apartment of someone who lives close by where at least one in the group will pass out. When she is on the street, she is at a loss as to what to do. She feels pulled back to the Towers, as if she needs new proof that it really exists and is not just a strange dream inspired by *Hiroshima, My Love* and whatever other random bits and pieces that ended up in the blender of her brain. As she starts walking toward the metro station, she wonders vaguely if this compulsion has more to do with the Towers being real for her specifically; that it has had a real impact, that her world, no matter how insignificantly, has changed. Her thoughts stop there; the alcohol in her system does the job it is meant to do.

She takes her time, stops in a café for a quick coffee, aims for a light fogginess in her head by the time she arrives. Once she has exited the metro, she is reassured by the eerie whiteness that greats her. Her thoughts manage to gain some traction with the idea that she might lose her mind, which is to say all measure of what is broadly real, if she works in the central office for long enough. She is undoubtedly hastening the loss because it is easier to just not think about much of anything, work related or not. Perhaps that is a touch melodramatic, similar—only less poetic—to imagining Hiroshima in the square.

On that note, she walks to the square, where a temporary market creates a massive dark splotch in the middle of the white. The stalls mainly offer fabrics, for the most part somber and muted, but with flashes of color here and there occasionally making it all the way up the scale to garish. She wanders through it, idly looking for a material with the same light channeling thread as Andesmas's suit. Her focus shifts to a mother and son, who is probably around Albert's age—she is not exactly well versed in the physical characteristics of different ages of children—both wearing clothes on the dreary side of the spectrum. She follows them at a discrete distance. The boy is mostly interested in looking under the tables, into the mysterious spaces behind the skirts. Natalie suspects that, if his mother was not holding his hand, he would disappear in an instant. The mother is drawn in by tastefully colored fabrics, pausing to run her free hand across them before moving on. She doesn't buy anything.

Natalie's fog slowly clears, though she is still not in the state of mind to speculate about the repercussions of this activity on her theory of the lifelessness of the square. The only thought that comes to her is that it reinforces the idea that the Towers will never be a perfect museum piece with people still living here. Beyond that, she is tempted to crawl behind one of the skirts herself. She imagines that there are piles of soft, warm fabrics there and that the darkness would make the colors meaningless. She wonders if the real Albert was like this; he clearly had his own world, but the world seemed to be all about adventure and spectacle. That sort of world is also attractive to her, in its own way.

She decides to leave the square and head to the apartment building of Albert's family. She finds it easily enough, but has no idea what number to put into the intercom. The list of names means nothing to her; she is fairly sure that André never mentioned their family name, but, even if he did, she would likely have forgotten it. After a moment, she crosses the street, finds a flat surface, fishes a pen and paper from her purse and scribbles Theo's name and address, as well as something about absences from school on it. Then she smudges his last name, the unit number and random areas of the message. When she notices someone, an older woman, about to enter the building, she approaches her.

"Hello," Natalie says.

The woman jumps, then looks back at her with suspicion.

"I'm sorry to bother you, especially at this time of night. My name is Natalie, I'm with the Ministry of Education. I'm here to check up on a student, Theo, who's been absent from class of late."

"This is highly unusual," the woman responds.

"I know, and I could get in trouble for coming here. It's just that Theo lost his brother quite recently. Following official procedure, with the number of days Theo has been absent, he would be taken into state care. Losing both her children would be very hard on his mother. I was hoping to have a conversation with the family before formal steps are taken, to see if there is a way to correct this and not break up the family."

"What do you want from me?"

"I wrote the details down on a piece of paper before coming here, but they've been smudged." Natalie hands the paper to the woman before continuing. "I don't know which unit they are in."

"I presently lead the association of residents for the building."

"You can help me, then? I'd be very grateful."

"We have given Miriam a lot of support."

"Solidarity is very important."

"Our community has held together, even as the neighborhood has fallen apart."

"I'm sure that you have worked very hard."

"It only happens by working together on common projects, projects that benefit everyone."

"I absolutely agree."

"We paint the lobby and hallways regularly as a group. Because it is white, it takes an extra effort to keep the common areas looking fresh and clean."

Natalie barely stops herself from saying that everything looked spotless the last time she was in the building.

"Residents used to paint the Towers together. They went to work together. They lived everyday together, as a community. Now, the government has to hire painters from who knows where to keep the Towers clean. There are no more jobs here; everyone just comes back to sleep. But, in our building, we still have a community."

"I'm very sorry to hear that. For the neighborhood, I mean."

"Miriam has always been very proud and independent. She did not think that she needed anyone's help. We nonetheless supported her when her little Albert passed on."

"Community is important."

"She has never joined us in painting the common areas."

"That is unfortunate."

"It does not surprise me that she is allowing Theo to run wild. He takes after his mother; no respect for others, always the lone wolf."

"He is only nine." Natalie is shocked to find that she remembers something André said.

"He needs to be in school, otherwise he will never learn."

"I agree. It sounds like he can also benefit from the association you've created here. I'm not sure that state care will give him a better model."

The woman nods resolutely. "Yes, the Committee does an excellent job, however the state cannot help but be impersonal."

There is a pause in the conversation. Natalie is not quite sure if it is heading where she thinks it is heading.

"When you talk to Miriam about Theo and school," the woman continues, "talk to her about the importance of the community. I don't like that you are not following the rules, but, well, this is probably for the best. We all felt the loss when Albert passed; he gave the building more positive energy than one of the stained-glass windows on a sunny day."

She opens the door and holds it for Natalie. "They are in unit 806."

"I promise to do my best to communicate to Miriam just how significant working together is," Natalie says as she walks by. "Thank you very much for your help."

"We are all in this together. If Theo loses his way, our society will be the worse for it."

"Very true," Natalie replies, even though she can see that the woman is no longer paying attention. She is completely absorbed in a careful inspection of the lobby. Natalie imagines that she does this every time she goes through the space, and is the sort of person who will harangue everyone else if she finds even the smallest thing out of place.

Natalie quickly goes to the elevator, worried that the woman will realize that something is not right and ask for proof that she really works for the Ministry of Education. When the door closes, she takes a deep breath. She notes that her fog has utterly vanished and that she is once again in her crazy dream world. Even without the seafood, impersonating a Ministry official just to have a few words with a nine-year-old boy that she scared off at a back alley puppetry show seems to her completely unreal. This is the sort of thing she would have imagined doing when she was a teenager, before her parents signed the charter.

She pauses at the door, worried that once she commits herself by knocking, she will be sucked into the personal world of the family. With André, at least she had a shield. He would be the one interacting with people and would give her something safe to look at. She takes another deep breath. If her take on the woman who let her in is correct, she will probably come up to check that nothing untoward is happening as soon as she is done in the lobby. With that unsettling though, Natalie knocks with make-believe authority.

Two minutes later, Miriam opens the door a crack and peaks out.

"Yes?"

"Hello, my name is Natalie Chaulieu, with Public Health. We met the other day with my colleague, André."

"What do you want?" Miriam sounds fearful, as if Natalie is at the door as a representative of the state, there to take her away after its investigation confirmed what she has already taken as a foregone conclusion; that she was a terrible mother. It is doubtful that she is scared for herself, since she would believe that any punishment would be justified. If she were taken away, however, she would also be a failure for Theo. The fear changes to confusion when she notices that Natalie is alone.

"I'm sorry to bother you this late. When we came before, Theo was not here. I was wondering if I could have two words with him, if he is home. It will only take a moment."

Miriam looks at Natalie, prepared to be defiant. Then her shoulders collapse and she opens the door wider, as if she no longer has confidence that she is capable of making the right decision. She calls over her shoulder for Theo. He joins them at the door an instant later, clearly having been standing just around the corner listening in on the conversation. Natalie flashes a smile, which she hopes does not come off as an off-putting grimace and squats down in front of Theo.

"Hi Theo. My name is Natalie Chaulieu, as you probably heard. We crossed paths at the puppetry show the other day. I just wanted to come here and introduce myself. I am going to be there tomorrow. I don't want you to think that you have to stay away because of it."

"Okay," Theo says.

Natalie rises and addresses Miriam.

"Thank you for your time."

"I don't understand."

"It's just as well. Have a good night."

Natalie walks back to the elevator, leaving Miriam and Theo in the doorway. Maybe she could have done more, actually asked questions, that sort of thing. That would have been beyond what she was prepared to do. So, she is stuck with the possibility that Theo might go to the marionette show tomorrow, and the obligation for herself to be there.

Chapter 9

George lets himself into Natalie's apartment and starts to make breakfast for the two of them. Natalie, still in bed, hears him and realizes that it must be Saturday. She curses; not only did she do work in the evening, she is obliged to continue on the weekend. She should have known that yesterday was a Friday, if only by the size of the group that went to the bar after work. She just went through the motions automatically; such details did not cross her mind. At least work would consist of a puppet show and potentially a quick conversation with Theo. It would not be horrible or soul crushing, only strange and awkward.

"Late night last night?" George asks rhetorically as he brings a tray with eggs, toast, coffee and lemon tea into the bedroom.

"Actually, no."

"Are you feeling unwell?"

"The eternal question."

George sits on the bed and picks at the eggs.

"Good news," he declares. "The filming is done. Postproduction will be at the studio, so I am going to be in the capital for the foreseeable future. I can already feel my general level of frustration and anxiety falling off. So, not only will I be around more, I will be far less grumpy."

"The project hasn't changed, though."

"No, it's true. And I still see their faces, hear their voices pretty much every day. But not being there makes a difference. I can distance myself, get lost in the technique, in constructing a coherent story. I do feel guilty sometimes. I mean, are they going to become less real, less human to me? Probably, especially with the story that I am in charge of shoehorning them into. But, whatever; that sort of guilt leads nowhere good. Just focus on the technique and making you breakfast."

"Why don't you make two versions?"

"I . . . I hadn't actually thought much about that. Instinctively, I'd say that the risk is too high. The studio is pretty tightly monitored. And I'm not sure that people will care. Not even the workers themselves care that their jobs are killing them. On the other hand, just for myself, to feel that there is an ounce of integrity left in me; no, the risk, it isn't worth it."

"Maybe you shouldn't decide immediately."

"Yeah, maybe. So, it's Saturday, life is passably pleasant, the world hasn't ended; what do you want to do today?"

"I have to work."

"I'm not sure that I understand what you just said."

"I have to work. I'm not sure how long it will take. We can do something later, I can call you or you can stay here."

"I'm sorry; work, today? Are you doing emergency or security stuff now? Can you even tell me?"

"No, nothing like that. It's . . . I didn't realize that today was Saturday, I sort of set up a meeting. He might not even be there; I could be back in an hour."

"So you can tell me the details? Because you are acting kind of strange, stranger than usual."

"You won't believe me. I am meeting, or, well, nothing was really set up; I promised someone that I would be at a puppet show today and sort of obliquely suggested that he should come."

"That doesn't sound like work."

"It's a nine-year-old that we've been having trouble tracking down. His brother died in the recent outbreak and he might have some information."

"We?"

"The public health guy I've been working with in the Towers."

"It was his idea? He's going to be there?"

"No, I just sort of did it."

"Okay, wow. You know that this sounds as if you care, right?"

"I'm aware."

"And you are well known for your warm and friendly way with

81

kids."

"I did scare him away the first time."

"I do believe you, by the way. You're acting strangely, but it isn't as if you haven't imagined crazier things. It's probably the influence of your pet apocalyptic utopia."

"Yes, probably."

Natalie sips some tea and eats a slice of toast. Then she leaves the comfort of the bed and gets ready for the day.

"Does a puppet show mean that you will be free to wear something a little less drab?"

"Probably."

George continues to pick at the eggs, pours himself a cup of coffee and observes Natalie whenever she is in sight. After a certain time in the bathroom, she goes to the wardrobe and immediately picks out one of the variants of the insipid amoeba costume.

"Not that I doubt your ability to make friends with a child, but maybe I will stick around here for a bit."

Natalie shrugs and heads to the door.

"Of course, a goodbye kiss for your boyfriend would give me more confidence," George calls after her.

She pauses for half a second, then continues without a word or looking back. She hears George yell, "I love you, too," as she is closing the door.

Natalie arrives at the alley in the late morning. She never asked when the show began, so she is thankful yet disappointed to see the two puppeteers setting up. It doesn't make sense to her to be nervous about coming here and her possible conversation with Theo, but she still feels it. She approaches the stage and says hello. They poke their heads up, as young and carefree as they appeared the first time.

"Sorry again for scaring away your audience last time," Natalie continues. "Have they come back?"

"Not all of them," one answers, "but most. We should have a less skittish group today, including adults and families. It being the weekend and all."

"Did you know that you have a cop following you?" the second asks.

"No, I wasn't aware." Natalie goes to the side of the stage and pretends to look at a marionette so she can see the person following her. A male insipid amoeba is standing next to the wall at the entrance to the road, opposite the faucet. She suddenly wonders if it's weird to give a gender to a hermaphroditic creature, then imagines how much she would have to change to transform him into a woman. After concluding that it would really only require removing the tie, changing the shoes and growing the hair a bit, she turns to the second puppeteer.

"How can you tell? They—we, really—all pretty much look the same. And, in my experience, the police are reluctant to leave their cars."

"They don't use cars around here. The alley might be too tight. Anyway, they all do the same thing; hang around at the intersection. Sometimes they come in to have a chat, or walk by to confirm the identity of an audience member, but then they'll go back. They want people to know that they are here, watching them, but they don't want to get in the way or interact more than necessary."

"You're not concerned?"

"No, especially not on a weekend. This is good wholesome entertainment for citizens who want to stay out of trouble. Besides, he's clearly here because of you."

The audience, consisting mainly of families with younger children, begins to arrive. They maintain a respectful distance from the policeman, all the while making sure that he can clearly see who they are. Natalie has never seen anything quite like it, likely because she is not in the habit of partaking in wholesome entertainment. Unlike her first time here, when the kids just sat on the bare ground, the audience treats the show as a more formal outing. They pull out blankets and pillows; some even have food.

"This is quite the community gathering," Natalie observes.

"Why not hold it in the central square?"

"The square is too big; it feels impersonal," the first puppeteer responds. "If we were more important, maybe it would make sense, but we want to stay small."

"We would need a tent and other equipment," the second adds. "That costs money, attracts unwanted attention, creates all sorts of additional headaches. Maybe once we're done school, if we're unlucky enough to not find a permanent indoor theatre. You should go sit down, we are about to begin."

Natalie scans the crowd for Theo, but does not see him. The policeman is still on the corner, so she wonders if any of the street urchins will take the chance to watch the play. The first puppeteer welcomes everyone and announces that they are going to show the classic *Don Juan*. Natalie settles in at the edge of the crowd against the wall and makes a mental note to bring something soft to sit on if she ever comes again. Then she loses herself insofar as possible in the play, which proves almost as violent though much less random than the two marionettes running around trying to kill each other that she saw last time.

When the play is over, Natalie looks around again. The policeman is still at the corner and she can't see Theo in the audience. She racks her brain to figure out why the cop might be following her, but nothing special pops out. There are so many small things that she does that are at best unwise, she has too many to choose from. Andesmas's amoeba might have taken offense and used his influence to have her followed. The woman who let her into the apartment building might have called the police. If cops are on foot around here, they could have been at the synth-pop show. Someone at the office might have found it suspicious that she hasn't turned in the Tonda Keller file. The list is potentially endless.

She rises and quickly walks to the end of the street behind the stage, hoping that the policeman will have a difficult time making his way through the crowd in the middle of shaking out and packing their blankets. As soon as she turns the corner, she runs into Theo.

"You are here," Natalie says, stopping in her tracks.

Theo starts walking away. Natalie takes the liberty of joining him. She tries to prepare herself for the conversation. Her mind goes back to Hervé, her boss at the laundry. He was good with people; she just has to act like him.

"You aren't running away this time. That's an improvement."

"Mom said you know what happened to Albert."

"You probably know more than me; you were at his side."

"He was sick. Then he was gone."

They turn a corner.

"Did he draw the Squirrel King on the wall?"

Theo shakes his head.

"It was you, then?"

"I was trying to distract him."

"The King was your idea?"

He shakes his head again as they turn another corner.

"Where did it come from?"

"Him. He would make up stories. Especially after a marionette show. He thought they could be better. Alice and Jean encouraged him."

"But not you?"

"It was too much."

"Your mom said that you didn't mind having him around. That was really mature of you."

"I couldn't leave him alone. He was always dreaming. He almost got hit by a delivery truck a couple of months ago. Didn't even know he was walking into the street."

"When I was young, I always had my nose in a book. I can't count the number of times my sister stopped me from running into things. You were a good older brother."

Natalie wonders momentarily why she thought of Hervé before her sister. She tries to think of whether her sister was good at this sort of thing, but draws a blank.

"I couldn't save him," Theo says.

Natalie starts to panic, unsure of how to respond to that. She admonishes herself for not just sticking with Hervé.

"There are some difficulties beyond our abilities, unfortunately," she finally replies. "I bet that you look after your mother now."

"I don't know what to do. She doesn't know what to do. She used to know what to do. She decides, then she changes her mind, then she just does nothing. She couldn't even make dinner. She stood in the kitchen, frozen."

Natalie walks straight a couple of steps before she realizes that Theo turned another corner. She hurries to catch up to him again, glancing frequently at the ground so she doesn't trip.

"But it has gotten better, right?"

"A little. It comes back though."

"Wow, I didn't know. I mean, why would I know? But, that must be very difficult."

"It's better if I'm not there."

"Really? She doesn't worry about you?"

"Yeah, but then she doesn't have to choose."

Natalie is unsure about how to respond to the logic. It seems so wrongheaded; she can imagine his mother being worried sick every time Theo is out of sight, afraid that she will lose him too. She is probably just as concerned that she will overreact and smother him. Maybe Theo is right, though; on some level, she might feel a certain relief when he is someone else's responsibility. If that's the case, she is probably wracked with guilt for even thinking that. But Natalie doesn't really know much of anything, and channeling Hervé or anyone else isn't giving her any answers. She feels like the conversation is just leading her deeper into a minefield and that she is going to say something that will make Theo run off.

"We are trying to figure out how Albert got sick. I was hoping that you could help us."

"When she's gone like that, I pretend that she's just like Albert.

She's just imagining something fun. She's taking a break from dinners and the apartment and work."

"She said that you and Albert always left the house together in the morning. Could you show me where you went? How you got there?"

"And me."

"I'm sure your mother doesn't need a break from you."

"Why not?"

"I . . . I don't know."

"But she wasn't imagining anything. Or, at least, not like Albert."

"Why do you say that?"

They turn another corner.

"She was stuck. Albert always moved. Until the sickness, anyway."

Theo suddenly stops. Natalie takes another step before following suit. She looks around and quickly finds her bearings.

"We are in front of your apartment," she says matter-of-factly.

"You said that I should show you where we went."

"Yes, please."

"It's not always the same."

"I understand."

"We avoid cops."

"Why? Not that I think it's unreasonable in any way."

"Mom doesn't like cops."

"Fair enough."

"They are always talking to the principal."

"I'm not sure that missing school is the best choice, even with cops there."

Theo scrutinizes her.

"Not that I am in the position to say what you should or shouldn't do. I just want to get a better idea of what happened to Albert."

There is a pause, then Theo starts walking again. Natalie follows. They walk along what seems like every road and alley in the neighborhood. They can all be divided into a handful of types; the back or side of buildings with small or no windows, the back or side with large windows, apartment fronts and shop fronts. After over an hour of walking in silence, Natalie wishes that Theo would do something to distract her from her aching feet. When she was working for the laundry, she was used to being on her feet all the time. Office life has softened her. Eventually, they come to a corner where Theo stops. He looks carefully around the edge of the building.

"The cop from the show is gone," he says.

They walk around the corner to see another puppet show in progress.

"They do two shows on Saturdays?" Natalie asks.

"Sometimes. Usually when cops show up to the first show. Or if they want to try something new."

"And they are here all week long?"

"Not all the time. Lots, though."

"Makes one wonder when they have time for class."

"This is better than school."

"More entertaining, any . . . ah shit."

Natalie steps in the same puddle she walked through the first time she came down this alley. She comforts herself by saying that she is lucky she managed to not trip and fall on their seemingly endless trek.

"What's the faucet used for? It's strange that it's here; I don't think we passed another one."

"We did. Several. The painters use them."

"That makes sense. I guess whoever designed this place recognized the need to take care of the white walls. They didn't think that it would just stay the same for all time."

"I guess."

"Wait, did Albert ever drink from it?"

"We all do, sometimes. If we're thirsty."

"Around the time he got sick?"

"I don't remember. Maybe. But he didn't usually notice when he was thirsty."

"It's possible, though."

"Yeah."

"You should avoid drinking from it in the future."

"That's how he got sick?"

Theo stares disbelievingly at the faucet.

"We won't know until it is tested."

Theo doesn't respond. He looks like he is about to kick the faucet, but then his shoulders slump, just like those of both his mother and the mother of the other family she visited with André. Natalie tries to find a way to extirpate herself from the situation with a modicum of grace.

"Thank you very much for showing me around."

Natalie turns to leave.

"You aren't going to stay to watch the end of the show?"

"No, I have to go. You have been a great help. Thank you again."

"Yeah."

Theo walks slowly toward the audience, dragging his feet. Natalie watches him until he sits down on the bare pavement. She makes a mental note to give him a blanket if she ever sees him again. She then makes her way to the metro on her soggy, uncomfortable feet, stripping off her Hervé mental costume on the way. A thought lingers after the change; that Theo had somehow trusted her enough to be more open about his family than he had been to anyone else since the death of his brother. The idea seems to her highly improbable and, in any case, unhelpful now that she has the information she was looking for. What could she, a stray cog, have to offer a boy like that except a great example of someone not to be like?

Natalie is thankful as her thoughts move along. The notion of white faucets of death on every corner tickles her imagination. Not everyone can be in the epicenter of the blinding blast. It makes sense to liquefy that energy and distribute it evenly throughout the city. The corpses can be collected and drained with relative ease. Death can stay in her cabaret and profit from the modern convenience of running water and motorized delivery vehicles. And if the painters use the water, one could somewhat poetically say that the very walls of the city are painted with death. Pure, brilliant death that is refreshed every time it gets a bit shoddy and discolored.

By the time Natalie enters her apartment, Theo is but a distant memory. The interaction is distilled in a mental note to tell André about the faucet.

Chapter 10

"The problem was that none of the soldiers would drink the treated water," Hervé Marne explains. "But the idea was the right one and if it could work in the middle of trench warfare, where corpses of man and beast festered as far as the eye could see, it would work anywhere."

Natalie is standing with Andesmas and Marne beside a huge centrifuge in the heart of the water treatment plant. This is not what Natalie was expecting to do today, but the invitation she received this morning did not seem like something wise to refuse. The invitation did not indicate that she would be in such rarified company, which is off-putting. Happily, one of the upsides of the insipid amoeba costume is that it is useful for all occasions. She can hide behind it while she tries to figure out what is going on.

"You breathed putrescence, you could taste it, and that became normal. Death, misery, constant anxiety that the next shell or bullet would have your name on it, that you would be the next guy wailing that you can't feel your leg"—he taps his prosthetic leg with his cane—"or begging the medic for more morphine; all that became a part of daily life. Yet, you couldn't get used to the taste of chlorine in the water. A chemical that stopped you from a slow and horrible death from some disease—rationally, on some level, you knew that—but you couldn't bear drinking it. It seems absurd, but that was the reality that I was faced with."

Marne takes a long pause to let his words sink in. Natalie thinks back to what André had told her about Marne only finding a system that worked for clean water with minimal chemicals after the war. She wonders how he will spin it.

"With a great deal of hard work and patience, I succeeded in finding a better solution. The chlorine wasn't the problem, so much as the engineers dumping huge quantities of the stuff into the water. That was how much they needed to kill all the bugs, they said.

Well, they were right; that is exactly how much was needed for a standing vat of water. But, that is like dumping cream into a cup of coffee without stirring it. It seems obvious, I know! If the water was stirred, the same job could be done with less chlorine. The trick was finding the balance between the stirring—we were on a battlefield, so it wasn't as if I could just grab a mixer off the shelf and go to town with it—and the chemical—which was not intended for hare-brained experiments. And, it wasn't as if I could work in a peaceful lab."

He taps his prosthetic and pauses again for effect.

"What really motivated me was the thought of all the needless suffering; all those young men—boys, most of them—serving their country—a whole generation of patriots—laid up with fevers and uncontrollable diarrhea; all that suffering that I could help stop. Dying because you drank water from a shell crater where the corpse of a horse—yes, they still used horses—was slowly rotting away; that was a terrible and ignoble way to go. That pushed me to find the solution, the ideal balance. And, I did."

Another pause. Natalie is taken aback by the number of "I's" she hears. It is so far from how things work that it is difficult to process. She wonders if he is given a lot of leeway as a war hero, in a matter of speaking, but heroes are generally met with mistrust; there is always a suspicion that the hero is taking credit for the work of others, that he is narcissistic and vain. People like that are not conducive to social harmony and, as far as she knows, are generally put out to pasture or muzzled. Alternatively, they can rise to the top, carried by a cult of personality, as happened in the early, ideologically charged days of the Committee. Marne doesn't fit either profile. She wishes that she could remember more from his file.

She glances over at Andesmas, thinking that he must be nearing the breaking point, ready to call Marne out on his megalomania and have him sent to a re-education camp or the middle of nowhere. Instead, his expression shows a respectful patience completely absent in their first encounter. Of course, she is a nobody who has accomplished nothing in life, so it's not as if he would have had a compelling reason to curb his impulse to take the teabag out of her cup or to dismiss the beliefs of the server in the cabaret right in front of her. But, that's not how a model of society should have acted; it shouldn't have mattered whether she had some special worth or talent. It amuses her that he is just as weak as everyone else.

"Potable water with minimal use of chemicals. It became even more of a challenge after the war; the sensitivity of soldiers to the taste of chlorine was nothing compared to that of the general population. Scaling up the operation was also quite something. On the other hand, I didn't lose a limb doing it, so it couldn't have been that difficult."

Pause. Maybe clean water is so important that, because Marne is the only person with the expertise to keep the facility running, he gets a pass. It is hard to believe that there are no other engineers capable of doing the work, though. Every city in the country has running water and someone has to manage each system. The capital region undoubtedly has a higher profile, but the fundamentals are not different. Again, as far as she knows.

"Long story short; I succeeded there too. An average of two hundred and fifty million liters comes through the centrifuges every day to serve all the water needs for the region. Given usage trends and population growth, that will rise to three hundred and fifty in the next ten to fifteen years. The plant is ready for it. We have a bacteria rate that is the envy of all the capitals on the continent, and equipment can scale up to the population of some God awful third-world megapolis."

Pause. When it is clear that Marne has actually finished his story, Andesmas speaks: "Thank you for the invitation to see that plant. Clean water is something we tend to take for granted; we must not forget just how important it is for maintaining, and improving, our quality of life. I assume that the other members of the

Committee have been through here?"

"Yes. I am, as you can tell, proud of my facility. I enjoy sharing that enthusiasm."

"While I appreciate spending time with Ms. Chaulieu, I am wondering about the logic in inviting only the two of us. It does not seem like a very effective use of your time."

"I believe that an invitation was also extended to your assistant."

"True. The comment stands, I think."

"You and the charming Ms. Chaulieu have of late become involved in files that concern water and neither of you have had the pleasure of seeing how the sausage is made, so to speak."

"Well, thank you again for the opportunity. Correct me if I am wrong, but the plant is multi-stage, is it not? I am passingly familiar with the version from the city I come from, and—while it is far less impressive than what you have here—I recall that it had a more complicated process."

"Yes, while chlorination is by far the best process, I have added ozonization and sand-filtering stages. It was a question of being thorough, you understand. If I hadn't introduced them, I would not be able to tell you today that we have experience in all modern techniques for treating water and have—unsurprisingly enough—found the technique I perfected to be the superior method. As there is no harm in running the water through the full range of processes, I have left them in place, even if they are not especially useful."

"Being thorough is wise, particularly when unclean water could have disastrous consequences."

"I believe that we understand each other perfectly. There is, of course, one more step in the process: testing."

Marne leads Andesmas and Natalie to a lab with large windows overlooking the facility. They look through the window at several people hard at work.

"I do not assume that the water leaving the facility is safe; it is constantly and exhaustively tested to ensure that it is safe. I do not take my responsibility for providing clean water lightly. There is in fact no scenario where contaminated water—water that would make the fine residents of our region sick—could find its way into the pipes. I have seen too much death and suffering in the world to not be absolutely sure that my modest influence on people's lives is entirely positive. I was forced to make do during the war; I refuse to compromise now."

Natalie mentally slaps herself on the forehead. Somehow Marne saw her report or had someone close to André and the public health team. The presence of Andesmas precludes the latter, as far as she is concerned, so somehow he got his hands on the report. This is a pre-emptive effort to avoid even a shadow of suspicion that his precious plant could have something to do with the outbreak. Suggesting that water might be the culprit was a throwaway phrase that she now vaguely regrets including. Maybe Marne has covered something up and they will never know for certain the source of the contagion, maybe there will be another outbreak because of it.

Despite his small stature, she starts to think of Marne as the man in the mythic hippo suit. She imagines that instead of becoming sensitive to harm through his war experiences, he became numb to it. He overplays his megalomaniacal hero of war and water to keep people off the scent of his pathological indifference. It is fascinating to see him as dangerous and unpredictable, badly adapted to a drearily normalized society. The image doesn't really work, any more than death pouring out of the faucets in the Towers does, but it makes life more interesting. It's not as if the deaths caused by the outbreak have any special meaning that is minimized by imputing them to an unthinking or capricious act by an eccentric, ungainly beast.

The reality is clearly that Marne is politically very well connected and there is nothing unpredictable about his actions. He may be dangerous, but it is calculated and probably only used when necessary. His lie about getting the balance right between stirring and chlorine during the war, if what André told her was true, only served to strengthen his position after the war to implement a system that, as far as she can see, works quite well. It's not as if the region has had daily outbreaks over the past decades. If he is covering up the root cause of the outbreak, it is probably both because it would be more harmful for the entire population to suddenly doubt the cleanliness of what is coming out of the tap and because he has a squeaky clean, if odd, reputation to uphold. This seems to her to be a far more important issue than tainted seafood, though she is not exactly in the best position to judge. Regardless of probable reality, she still hangs the hippo suit on him. He doesn't fit in the amoeba-ox continuum and the hippo suit has been stored unused in her mind since the visit to the second family.

While her mind has been wandering, the tour has come to an end. She finds herself walking out with Andesmas, the first time since he lit up in the Towers that they have been alone together. He is just as grey and worn as when she first glimpsed him in the lobby of his apartment building, before he was able to harvest the energy from the square. He fits well into the continuum; a former ox who has over time moved over to, but has not yet reached, the amoeba side. They walk toward the entrance, both still processing the experience of meeting Marne.

"I am surprised that you didn't feel the need to make some off-color remark," Andesmas says, breaking the silence.

"That's funny. I am surprised that you didn't say something about him taking all the glory for what is evidently a group effort."

Silence. They reach the entrance, where Andesmas has an official car waiting.

"You've given up using the metro?" Natalie asks. "Are you still living in the Towers?"

"I still have the apartment in the Towers. Most nights I don't make it home, though. It is an enormous amount of work, just keeping the lights on."

"There isn't another Hervé Marne at the power station?"

"There was, more or less. Unfortunately, he was run over by a car a couple of months ago. He was bicycling to work, as he had done for thirty years, and one day he accidentally turned left instead of right. No one knows why. Everyone is important in our society—you included—and so everyone's loss is felt."

Natalie holds back from asking how Albert was important, and how that relates to the cover-up she is now convinced is happening.

"Marne is a character and our society would not be harmonious if everyone was like him," Andesmas continues. "It is better to focus on the plant. Symbols can be very important to rally people to a common cause. The challenge is to make sure that the symbol does not replace the real thing. Utopia is clean running water for everyone, it is feeling safe when one walks down the street, it is having a roof over one's head. It is everything we should be able to take for granted. It is not some idealized world where everything is perfect; people will still pass away, youngsters will still struggle with finding their place, and characters like Marne will always be a part of the mix."

"How is the counter-charter coming along?"

"It is progressing nicely, thank you. Although it is just 'the charter', reflecting the values the Committee and all citizens who have chosen to be a part of our common project hold dear. The previous document is, if anything is, the counter-charter, as it is counter to the values of our society."

Natalie counts to ten to avoid blurting out that, in that case, the principal value in the new charter must be systemic repression.

"I actually thought that I would have a more important role to play in it, after our discussion in the Towers," she says instead.

"You are working with people from public health, no?"

"Yes, on the typhoid outbreak."

"Do you think the project is worthwhile? Does it help make people's lives better?"

"Yes."

"Do you think that working on the charter is more worthwhile? Be honest, it's not a trick question."

Natalie chooses her words carefully. "If we find and eliminate the cause of the outbreak, it will have a more immediate impact on people than the charter. The two can't be directly compared, though."

"I will hazard a guess and say that you personally find it more worthwhile. You are not an expert, so you might not think that you contribute as much as the others. It is very important that someone keeps the Committee informed and," he looks at her for a moment, "I wager that you have found plenty of other ways to help."

Natalie wants to say something about the messed-up priorities of the Committee, focusing on seafood rather than people's lives, or about the leak of her report and Marne's hypocrisy. Instead, she shrugs.

"Your work advances the project, even if it is sometimes difficult to see it on the ground. Eradicating preventable diseases is a significant step forward. On top of that, you are happier doing that sort of work than you would be drafting language for a document that, as you say, will not have an immediate impact. So, it seems to me that you are in a good place for both you and everyone else.

"I have a meeting that I am already late for. It was a pleasure to see you again."

Andesmas gets into the back of the car, which starts moving a second later. Natalie stays at the entrance, watching until the car turns a corner and disappears. She reflects on how persuasive Andesmas can be as she pulls out her flask and takes a drink. At least Marne—with or without the hippo suit—is entertaining when he lies.

Chapter 11

Natalie orders her lemon tea and joins André at their usual table in Caskets. André is going back and forth between a large utility plan and a stack of paper that she takes as the test results. The plan is already marked with the homes of the infected, the school and other landmarks. He is in the middle of marking water lines as red or green, depending no doubt on whether the tests came back positive or negative.

"So, you got my note?" Natalie asks.

"About Theo? Yes. It was good information."

Natalie stirs the teabag, intending to stay silent until André has finished categorizing the lines.

"You aren't married," she states, breaking her resolve.

He doesn't respond.

She came home yesterday to an apartment cleaner than it had been since George had last gotten it in his head to go through the place, before his trips to the countryside for his current film. The first time he did it, she felt a twinge of anger, as if he was violating her space in the same way the police had more or less regularly done when they searched the family home when she was growing up. As with many things in life, she realized a moment later that it wasn't important; she didn't feel all that close to her stuff, anyway. There was no point, since there was always a chance that it would be confiscated and inspected by some random amoeba at central. Besides, she liked having a spotless apartment, even if she was too lazy to do such a thorough job herself.

"I had a tour of the water plant yesterday," she says. "I met the famous Hervé Marne. He is rather off-putting, but in an entertaining sort of way."

André looks up.

"Why were you at the plant?"

"I figure that my report was leaked. It seemed like a pre-emptive move to ensure that the plant would never be suspected."

"You put in your report that it was the water?"

"I wrote that it was the most promising lead, but that more work needed to be done. In retrospect, I recognize that it wasn't wise to include it. I should have kept with what we knew for sure."

"Yes, that would have been best."

André goes back to coloring water lines and Natalie's thoughts go back to George. They practically live together these days, which is fine. She has found it easy to ignore his comments about her penchant for the insipid amoeba suit, her flask and other minor things. He does not seem to expect much from her. It is, of course, just as well because she has very little to give. Still, the lopsided nature of the relationship is vaguely disconcerting.

"If I didn't know any better," Natalie says, "I would say that Marne is trying to hide something."

"He is hiding things."

"As in, the plant really is the source of the disease."

"It's not."

"It's not? You're sure?"

André turns the map around.

"Look. The pipes upstream from this small area of the Towers have clean water. Whatever is getting into the water, it is happening locally, not at the plant."

"So, Marne is just hiding his past, then?"

"There might be other things but, yes, his past."

"And there isn't a cover-up?"

"Maybe there is. It's not for this outbreak, though. At least, not yet."

"Huh. Well, that makes the situation less interesting."

André doesn't comment. Natalie finally takes a sip of her tea.

"What's the plan now?" she asks.

"We dig, test what's around the pipes."

"That will take another week or two?"

"A rig was booked when we first suspected, so no more than a week."

"What about the politics?"

"Aren't you supposed to handle that?"

"Right, but pretend for a moment that I'm not terribly good at it."

"The damage has been done. Limit your communication to the fact that the work is ongoing and that we are making progress. Avoid saying anything about water."

"That's it?"

André shrugs.

Even if she is forced to admit that Andesmas is right regarding both the worth of the project and the value of her contributions to it, the scarcity of those contributions does not exactly make the whole experience very fulfilling. She doesn't mean fulfilling in the nutritional sense, though; only in the sense that it occupies her time. It would perhaps be nice to be fulfilled morally, esthetically, financially, and on and on. Even without all that, something benign to put her mind to is important for avoiding madness. She would go back to the office, but the blood red files are not what she would consider benign.

"I guess I'll just leave, then," she says. "See you in a week."

André nods.

"I'll let you know if something comes up."

"I don't think that will be necessary."

"If Marne is as connected as he seems to be, who knows what strings he might pull."

"Okay."

Natalie gets up. Her thoughts are already at the clean apartment she will be going back to. There might even be food. Andesmas was right about paradise being the little things that one should be able to take for granted. George rarely does anything flashy, but his fundamentals are fantastic. On the other hand, the Towers has a certain poetry that, for her, is completely lacking in the Andesmas style utopia.

She leaves the cabaret and immediately spots a cop-like amoeba. He is probably the same as the other day, though she can't tell them apart. Just because she has the rest of the day ahead of her, she approaches him.

"Hi, how are you doing on this lovely day?" she opens.

"Ma'am," he replies with a slight nod.

"You've been following me for a bit. Or one of you; I can't tell you apart."

He doesn't respond.

"Is this the sort of thing where you can ask me a bunch of questions and we can get it all over with now, or should I expect a shadow from now on?"

"We can go down to the station now, ma'am. I can book you for interfering with an ongoing investigation. If that's what you wish."

"Wow, that's kind of twisted."

Natalie wants to ask him if Marne is behind the so-called investigation. She refrains, knowing that a cop stuck standing out here will have no idea where his orders originated from. Instead, she walks away. She contemplates losing him in the maze of streets or forcing him to stand for hours on end in the main square, but she can't be bothered. So, she heads straight home. On the street in front of her apartment, she sees the three black cars that are the usual sign of police surveillance.

When she enters the apartment, she is surprised to find George at the kitchen table with one of her bottles of whisky and a glass. Her hope of time alone in a clean apartment with food is dashed. She supposes that she has a responsibility to be supportive, as compensation for the domestic paradise. George, unlike her, is not prone to drinking in the middle of the day, so she might have her work cut out for her. It is probably just as well, since it will keep her mind off other things.

"Aren't you supposed to be editing your propaganda film?"

"It's cancelled. The government doesn't want it anymore."

"Did they tell you why?"

"No."

"Is that a celebratory drink? I mean, I know that you prefer celebratory pie, but it's been a rough project."

"Something must have happened."

"Such as?"

"I don't know. A factory exploded or something."

"You do realize that the Committee is pretty capricious when it comes to things like this. The smallest thing could have shifted their priorities."

"If that was the case, they would have shifted me to something else. Instead, they just told me to go home."

"They have all the footage?"

"Yes. The security at the studio is pretty tight."

"Did you start working on the second version?"

"No. It would be useless now anyway and the risk was too high."

"You should bake a pie and get your mind off it. There's nothing you can do."

George, who has just been holding a mostly full glass in his hand, drains it in one swallow. Then he grimaces as Natalie laughs.

"I get your frustration, but are you sure drinking is the answer?"

Bloody hell, she says to herself, *now I sound like him half the time he sees me pull out my flask.*

"Isn't that what you do, drink to stop thinking about things?"

"No, not really."

"Why, then?"

Natalie doesn't really want to get into why she drinks, so she stays silent. George pours himself another glass. Natalie goes to the cupboard, gets a glass and pours herself one too. Then she offers a toast.

"To crazy characters and common costumes."

She clinks George's glass with her own and takes a drink.

George, his thoughts suddenly elsewhere, mechanically lifts his glass to his lips, then lowers it without drinking.

"You are thinking about the people from the village," Natalie says.

"I lied before. I was trying to convince myself that things were easier being in the capital, not having to see them every day. Not having to drive out there every day, that has made things easier, I was dead tired by the end of it. But my conscience hasn't let up; I still know what's happening out there."

"You said that the villagers bought into it; they were proud of their work, felt a bond with the administration, were grateful that they could stay in the village and played down, even denied, their illnesses. You couldn't have fought against that and none of it was your fault."

"If I was a real filmmaker, I could have crafted something so powerful, so convincing; it could have changed everything. I didn't even try. Risks. Risk of what? Losing my membership? People are dying and that's all I think about. I am a horrible person."

George empties his glass once more. This time, he is too numb to feel it go down and Natalie no longer thinks that levity is the appropriate response.

"Yup," Natalie says. "Welcome to the club. It's peaceful, once you get used to it."

"At least you are helping people."

"I'm doing what, now? I am a liaison to the Committee—well, a sub-amoeba of the Committee—working with public health professionals. The public health folks help people, and then I inform the government. I tell the same people who ordered your propaganda film about the details and they can do whatever they want with it; minimize it, cover it up, sweep it under the rug, or whatever else they can think of. I guess that would fit under somebody's definition of helping others, but not yours."

"I didn't know."

"Clearly. It's not worth talking about; I am not in the position to do anything about it. So, let's focus on other things."

Natalie is displeased that the morose George has returned and that it looks as if there is no end to it in sight. She was just getting used to the idea of the happier version of him being generally around, viewing him in a way not categorically different from running water. The least he could do is to turn into someone more interesting when he is depressed; the self-pity is nothing if not tedious. Perhaps she should do more, but grandiose and outlandish ideas are more her strong suit. She is somewhat short on practicality and helpfulness.

"Besides sitting here, working at emptying the bottle," Natalie asks, "what would best take your mind off the cancellation of your film?"

"I don't even want to get up."

"You are trying to be like me. How about going back to Caskets? I will even brave the evil and condescending bouncer."

"I don't know. It's pretty far."

"It is another world. Travel time is to be expected. But, you know, it is another world."

"Fine."

George stays in his seat.

"Assuming that you haven't drunk too much, and I know you haven't, you will feel better just getting out of the house. And, with the overwhelming pinkness of the place, it won't matter what we wear."

"Yeah."

This time, George gets up. Natalie pulls out her flask and tops it up with brandy. Then they get ready to leave, Natalie choosing a light grey jacket with a hood. George is about to turn off the kitchen light when Natalie stops him.

"Let's just leave that on," Natalie says. "Then we won't have to fumble around in the dark when we get back."

Once they exit the apartment, Natalie guides George to the back stairs. He follows without asking questions and she does not bother giving an excuse. She doesn't want to tell him about the cop who's following her around, nor does she want to be followed to the cabaret. She puts her hood up when they leave the building and down again a couple of blocks later. She figures that her insipid amoeba getup is enough of a disguise for the police who are not specifically assigned to watch her.

The bouncer is the same, though this time he waves them in without comment. Natalie wonders if he remembers her due to her downtrodden look or if he is linked to the police. Ultimately, so long as getting in isn't a hassle, the reasons why are not terribly important to her. Avoiding obvious, targeted surveillance can be worth the effort; trying to evade all the watchers in a surveillance state is the definition of futility.

The interior is as pink as it was last time and the music is just as approximate.

"They have obviously listened to all the smuggled records from the London punk scene," George says.

"And you know this how?" Natalie asks rhetorically.

George manages to smile. He then turns to the stage and starts to lose himself in the music. Natalie orders drinks and then joins him. His eyes are closed, head bobbing to the beat. She holds on to the drinks, not wanting to disturb him. The songs, which rarely go over two and a half minutes, follow each other in quick succession. He is slowly pulled closer to the stage, his head bobbing turning to jumping and dancing. She stays behind, rapidly finishes one of the drinks and slowly sips the other.

Natalie is less entranced by the music, falling out of the fantasy every time there is a jarring change of rhythm. Finding the visual environment more absorbing, she looks around at the other patrons. Andesmas can say what he will about the practicality of a subtle, understated sort of utopia, she would prefer that society aimed for a harmony of pinks rather than greys. Then she tries to imagine Andesmas in pink. In his special suit, he would come off like a sign for a strip club. Without it, some sort of pink-hued rock worn by millennia of wind and rain. Either would be quite lovely, relatively speaking. She starts to imagine Marne pulling up his pant leg to reveal a pastel pink prosthetic when she sees the two puppeteers at a discrete booth, away from the stage. Her first instinct is to ignore them, her second to say "hello." She feels the need to distract herself from miserable George, just as he needs to be distracted from his film.

She swears that Theo mentioned their names, but she can't remember. She approaches the booth anyway, with a "I love your puppetry work." They invite her to join them, though it is clear that they can't immediately place her.

"You were saying that you study under Tonda Keller," she says.

"We wish," the first says. "We have had some classes with him, but it is rare that he directly supervises students."

"It is probably just as well," the second points out. "He is a staunch traditionalist. He is brilliant, but doesn't exactly appreciate new techniques. In the long run, it's better for us to be more flexible, so that we can always connect with the audience.

"We have certainly had to adapt for street theatre," the first continues. "That has been a huge challenge actually, because the more experimental graduates have been more likely to leave the country. So, innovation is not exactly encouraged."

"Do you have children?" the second asks. "Families make up most of our audience."

"No, I don't. I was introduced to your show by Theo," Natalie responds.

"How do you know Theo?"

"Through tragedy, I'm afraid. I have been looking into the death of Albert."

As soon as Natalie says it, she imagines that Death is at the counter, heard her words and is now looking over, blearily but intently. It is strange to mention a real and recent passing at the regional epicenter of wars and plagues.

"The Squirrel King," the first says sadly.

"King Squirrel the First," the second corrects the first with the same melancholic tone.

"Sorry to bring it up," Natalie says.

"We asked," the second replies.

"It was the blue gopher who was the hero, wasn't he?" the first asks.

"Champion more than hero; multi-gold medalist at the Olympic games of shiny objects. The games where the sports were their own reward."

Natalie looks over at the counter and jumps when she sees George standing next to her.

"That's an odd reaction," George comments.

"Yeah, sorry."

"Can I steal Natalie away from you ladies?" George asks the puppeteers.

They nod and Natalie follows George to a spot by the bar.

"I have it," George says. "The solution."

"Okay," Natalie replies with skepticism.

"What are you doing tomorrow?"

"There is more testing to do, which I am not a part of, so nothing specific. I should go into the office. What do you have in mind?"

"We have to go to the village and see for ourselves what's really going on."

"I'm not sure that I need to be there."

"I know that it's a lot to ask, but I need you. I don't think I can handle seeing a crater where the houses used to be if I'm alone. You are so much stronger than I am."

"That's just the alcohol."

George looks are her and takes her hands. Natalie wonders how far this whole support thing will have to go.

"Fine," she finally says. "On one condition: you have to make a serious effort not to mope when we come back, regardless of what we find."

"I'll do my best," he says, relieved. "Thank you."

He hugs her tightly and then they head home. Natalie waves at the puppeteers as they leave. She reflects on their tendency to never stay in the pink-hued version of the cabaret for very long.

Chapter 12

Natalie rarely took road trips as a child. She remembers a story a friend of her dad used to tell about a trip her family took to the northern mountains. She must have been very young or not born yet, and her parents never mentioned it. They were driving with the three black cars following along. Her dad was apparently frustrated, not so much that the police were following, but that the government was wasting so much money doing it. When they had stopped at a service station to fill up, he went to talk to the police. He suggested that one or even two join us in our car, explaining that it would be a far more efficient way to keep tabs on us and that there had to be far better things to spend the money for the gas for three cars on. The police apparently politely refused and continued to waste money.

While she was able to slip away from the police to head to the cabaret, it was not possible to do the same when leaving town in a car. Fifteen to twenty years have passed, and the police are still wasting money with their three black cars. George hasn't asked why they are following them; he is well aware of the routine, but can't be sure whether they are there because of him or her. Maybe he has assumed that he is the target, which makes sense if it turns out that the idyllic village he was filming is now a crater and the government wants to control that information. That would certainly be more relevant and less frivolous than the police following because of the throwaway line about water being the possible source of the typhoid outbreak. On the other hand, given how ridiculous and wasteful the Committee tends to be from time to time—one just has to look at how many resources they are throwing at the counter-charter—she would not dismiss out of hand her being the target. It was easier growing up, at least before her parents signed the charter; her dad was the only member of the family the police were interested in. Of course, the cops could be following both of them, though she's not sure they could accomplish such a feat without six cars.

The trip is made in silence. All sorts of scenarios are undoubtedly playing through George's mind. He did pack his K-3 camera and other film equipment, so he could try to record whatever they find. She wonders how far he would get before the police would intervene. She makes an effort to think of ways to distract them, but doesn't come up with any useful ideas. One of the upsides of having three cars is that it is difficult to distract or disable all of them.

"How far is it?" Natalie asks.

"About an hour."

"What are we going to do about the police?"

George shrugs. Neither of them have much to say. She wishes that the radio worked, just to fill the silence. That, along with most things in life, would be too much to ask for. Instead, she closes her eyes and, despite not feeling tired, tries to take a nap.

She wakes with a start to George shaking her shoulder.

"The valley is just up ahead," he announces, nodding toward the north.

"It looks fairly green and intact from here."

"It's not Hiroshima."

They wait until they are closer before commenting further.

"The buildings are still there," George says, with some relief. Natalie imagines him crossing his worst scenario off his mental list.

"Wait, what's that?" she asks, pointing to a light-colored blob in a pasture. "Is that a dead cow?"

"Yeah, it looks like it." George slows the car as they go past.

They reach the village, where it looks like people are going through their usual routine.

"It's weird," George says. "I would swear that everyone is moving slower than they did before."

He goes through the town and continues north to the industrial cluster.

"There's more dead livestock," Natalie points out.

The countryside is littered with dead livestock. There aren't that many, just enough to be noticeable.

"That's not normal," George says.

He turns the car around before they reach the dead zone around the factories. They are close enough for Natalie to see it for the first time. If there were a scene that was the diametric opposite of the main square in the Towers, this would be it. There is some black, around what she takes to be the power plant, but most of the area, the buildings and the ground where nothing grows, is a sort of indeterminate darkness. It is as if complete blackness would require a purity that the area lacks. This would be an appropriate home for Death, even if there are probably not enough people, or other animals, around to sate her thirst for blood. That is the great irony of the dead zone.

"Let's go see to the mayor," George says. "He likes to talk."

They head back through the village and stop at a small, nondescript house.

"I was expecting a hall of some sort," Natalie says.

"He doesn't like the hall, finds it undignified. It is literally a hall; no offices or anything like that. His official desk is tucked in a corner."

"Ah."

They get out of the car and go to the door. She notes that George isn't bothering with his camera, but doesn't question it. He knocks and, as they wait for someone to answer, they watch with amusement as the three black cars try to find spots in the cramped street where the house can be observed but where they are not causing a nuisance for the locals. It is almost touching how courteous they try to be. A couple of minutes later, a large man with a reddish complexion answers. He appears happy to see George again and immediately invites them in. He seems continuously out of breath, which might be ordinary as far as Natalie knows.

"You seem to be a bit out of breath, Tom," George says. "Is everything all right?"

Tom is busy in the kitchen, boiling water for tea and slicing cake. George sits on a couch in the living room; Natalie follows his lead.

"Just a moment," Tom calls from the kitchen.

Once everything is prepared, he slowly comes into the living room with a large tray and places it on the coffee table. Then he collapses in an armchair across from the couch, as if he has just climbed a mountain. He catches his breath, which, conveniently enough, is about the time needed for the tea to properly steep—as opposed to what Natalie prefers. He then pours three cups and offers cake.

"You missed a freakish fog," Tom says. "It would have made your film really dramatic. Or not, maybe it would have come out like a dark yellow-grey wall. Still, it was quite something. We are still recovering. It was so hard to breathe. Sam and Petunia"—he addresses Natalie specifically—"they were some of our community's most vulnerable members, they didn't make it through."

"What did the doctors say?" George asks.

"Respiratory issues, concentrations of sulfur dioxide. We should . . . excuse me."

Tom pulls out a handkerchief and coughs wheezily into it.

". . . We should be breathing normally in a couple of weeks."

"Sulfur dioxide? Isn't that from the zinc plants?"

"Sure."

"So it's a chemical from the industry in the north of the valley that just killed Sam and Petunia, as well as a bunch of livestock, I'd wager?"

"George, let's not get into this again. I enjoy your company, but your stance against industry is a position against all of us who work in the factories. And I'm being polite here."

"I know. It's just that people died. I can't just ignore that."

"Might as well get all bent out of shape the next time the river floods, or there's an earthquake or tornado. Maybe in the city you can pretend that these things don't happen, but out here . . . It's like when city folk are shocked at a cow being butchered but have no problem eating a steak."

"Wait, you are blaming it on the weather? And then you are saying that death happens, so it's okay?"

"Three days of fog so thick, you couldn't see your hand in front of your face. The air didn't move an inch. If that's not the weather, well, I'm just not sure what to say. Another slice of cake?"

Natalie takes a slice, while George shakes his head. She would like to pull George to the side and remind him that he now knows what happened here and why the film was cancelled, and that they can go. She understands, though, that this needs to play out. George needs to feel that he has done all he can to push the villagers to act or else he will be remorseful later. If he gets it into his head that she was the one who stopped him from trying, he will also resent her for it. So, she contents herself with the cake and insufficiently strong and bitter tea.

"Yes, of course that part is the weather. It is also evidence what the chemicals industry is pumping out can kill people. You can use this to improve conditions for everyone."

"It's easy enough to say, but we are all in this together." Tom pauses to cough into his handkerchief. "People here rely on the jobs at the factories. That is the only thing keeping this village going. If we suddenly demand that filters be added to protect us from a once in a lifetime event, the expense alone could make the plants go under. We're not making luxury goods here."

"The chemicals affect you every day."

"Yes, well, I think we can survive a bit of a cough."

"They are slowly killing you."

"Life does that. Do you think that laboring in the fields, taking care of the livestock, will make us live forever? Do you think that living in your city, cut off from the country, is healthy? Pick your poison."

"What about the livestock, all the cows that died?"

"The government is going to reimburse us. They have an emergency fund for natural disasters."

"So, there is money. Why can't you use that for the filters? They are government factories, after all."

"The government may own them, but they belong to the community. They need to be self-sufficient; otherwise, what's the point of having them at all?"

George does not reply, unsure about what other argument he can use.

"Look," Tom continues, "I understand you care about what happens here and that is why you are so insistent. It doesn't bother me much to have these sorts of friendly chats. We also appreciate that the Committee has noticed what we've accomplished here, balancing off the traditional way of life with modern progress. You are playing a big role in getting the word out, that living like sardines in the city is not a prerequisite for factory work; you should be proud of that. The very fact that you thought enough of us to check in after the fog says a lot about your character.

"That said, most folks around here find what you have to say condescending and I imagine that the black cars outside means that the government is under the impression that you might be going too far, stirring up trouble. So, take care of yourself, and have enough confidence in us to believe that we can do the same."

"The film has been cancelled."

"What?"

"That's the reason I'm out here. The film was cancelled and I didn't know why. Nobody outside the valley knows about the fog."

"Nobody really needs to know about the fog. Honestly, I would find it hard to believe had I not lived through it. And, we should probably dispose of the dead livestock before we are at the center of attention. I don't understand why they would cancel it, though. Why wouldn't they just delay the release?"

"You do realize that it's a propaganda film, right? Even before the film, I had a devil of a time cutting out images and sounds of sickness—especially the cough—while keeping a coherent narrative. With a couple of deaths, caused by the same chemicals that are making people sick, that wouldn't come off very well, no matter how long the release was delayed."

"Focusing on what works in our village rather than the compromises is not propaganda, it is just a light, feel-good film that reflects how we all already see things. You tend to be needlessly cynical sometimes, George; a sickness of the city, no doubt. Still, I suppose that there is a risk that the story is hijacked by the disaster; it is the most dramatic event that has happened in quite some time, and it is a sad fact that many of our fellow citizens are attracted by such tragic drama. The government is in a better position than we are to judge such things, however. Cake?"

Both Natalie and George refuse politely.

"Are you a filmmaker as well?" Tom asks Natalie.

"No, a puppeteer," Natalie lies. "Well, apprentice puppeteer."

"That's an interesting choice. You know, when I was a child there used to be travelling puppet shows that came from town to town. We were so excited when one came here—that was a dramatic event worth talking about. Now all we have is television, which, if you ask me, is just not the same. For a live show, you have to go into the city. There was one show that I remember like it was yesterday . . ."

Natalie and George let Tom talk. For her, the story is part of the natural flow of the conversation. Judging by the look of discouragement on George's face, he takes it as a way to end the argument and move on. He is not ready to move on, but that does not change anything. Tom is energetic, clearly very attached to memories of his childhood in the village. He has to stop from time to time to catch his breath and cough, which he takes in stride.

She has another slice of cake and reflects on her childhood. It was fine, happy enough. She just doesn't feel the same intimate connection that Tom does. The first thing that comes to her mind is a series of books she was reading about the time her parents signed the charter. The series was interminable, yet somehow she made her way through it. What strikes her is that, during the first third, the author had a tendency to talk about the poetry of everything; the poetry of a street, a face, a gesture. Everything in life had this sort of magical quality, a quality she didn't like at the time because it seemed to mean that nothing was special. When she started running around the capital, picking up laundry, she started to recognize and appreciate the poetry of the mundane, of misery, of all sorts of things that were not so magical. The poetry was how the author saw the world, it was his connection to it, it was the portion of the world he was driven to describe in his books. Although she didn't write, she started to feel—or, at least, imagine—the same sort of link. Then, after the first third, the author stopped writing "the poetry of." It was such a minor thing; the reader could still ascribe it even if it wasn't explicit. She didn't, though. Even if everything else about the writing remained the same, she assumed that the connection was lost, that the author no longer saw the world in the same way. That is how she feels about her childhood; she no longer sees the poetry in it, any more than she sees the poetry in her family or much of the world. Now, she only sees poetry in very special cases, such as the main square of the Towers. She doesn't consider this change to be good or bad, though it makes it difficult to relate to Tom's passion.

By the time Tom finishes his story, George has made up his mind to leave the village behind, insofar as he can.

"You know," George says to Tom. "I am happy that you are able to stay in your village and live the life you think worthwhile. Thank you for having us and for letting us know what happened. I was really worried. I expected to find a crater where the valley used to be."

"Can you finish the film anyway?" Tom asks. "It could be just for the village, something that reminds us of all we have to be

Chapter 13

Natalie has been expecting the authoritative knock on the door since the police surveillance started. The only question is whether they are here to search her place or take her to central for a cup of coffee, as the friend of her dad used to say. A search would be less of a hassle, but an interrogation might fill in some gaps in her theories. The two inspectors at the door ask her to follow them. She does without question, and after a quick ride in one of the black cars, she finds herself at central. Going through the building is a surreal experience since all the buildings in the cluster have the same floor plan and the furniture is standardized. She ends up in a room exactly like the small boardroom, after passing through the same sort of open office area where she typically works. The only obvious difference is that all the files are navy blue.

Although she has never been through an interrogation herself, she knows that the best response to any question is "I refuse to testify." Anything else will end up in the blue files, which will be put together with all the other information available in the red files and analyzed by people like her. Offhand remarks that are innocent in isolation can be joined with something one said ten years ago and a book bought sometime in the middle to create a damning story. If one starts from the premise that everyone is guilty and has access to details on all aspects of a person's life, proving that guilt is not that difficult. The problem for her is that she knows that she lacks the self-control to keep saying, "I refuse to testify," over and over, regardless of what buttons the investigators push.

"Thank you for joining us, Ms. Chaulieu," the first inspector says. "We just have a couple of routine questions. If you cooperate, you will be out of here in no time."

"Would you like a cup of coffee?" the second asks.

"Can I have a lemon tea?" Natalie asks.

"I'll see what we can do."

The second inspector leaves the room.

"We might as well start, if you don't mind," the first says. "You went out to the Seume Valley yesterday. Please explain why you were there."

"I was there to see the zinc."

"The zinc?"

"There is zinc in the valley, is there not? I went to see it."

"And did you manage to see the zinc?"

"No."

"Why is that?"

"The cows got in the way."

"In the way of what?"

"The zinc."

"Okay. You stopped by the village of Vantze and spent time with the mayor. Why did you spend time with the mayor?"

"To eat cake."

"And what did you talk about?"

"Cake."

"We have reason to believe that you were involved in subversive activities when you were there. Would you like to talk about that?"

"The cake was good."

The second inspector comes back with a black tea in a paper cup. He places it in front of Natalie.

"I was unfortunately unable to find lemon tea. I hope this will suffice."

They continue to question her about her trip with George and she continues to answer with a mix of zinc, cake and cows. She tries to answer in a way that isn't really a lie, but is entirely unhelpful. Then they switch tracks and start to question her about the Towers and the typhoid investigation. Here they ask more leading questions, such as "Why are you trying to use the outbreak to destabilize the country?" She doesn't have a good half-truth to give, so she goes with "The Towers is white," "The Towers is painted," "The Towers is bright" and so on. While she is sure that her answers can be twisted in myriad ways, occupying her mind by coming up with different adjectives lessens the risk that she blurts out something stupid or damning. She also appreciates that they lead to fewer follow-up questions, unlike the zinc-style responses she gave earlier.

A whole section of the questioning revolves around the conspiracy that she has cooked up with André and, occasionally, Helen. She starts to see a pattern, based on names included and excluded. The Seume Valley questions included the mayor but never touched on George. The Towers questions haven't included Andesmas, his pet amoeba, Marne or Theo—at least, not up until now. The interrogation turns to her relationship to a man she only figures out after the fact is the ranting father of the second family she visited with André and their efforts to sabotage the plant he works at. There are so many questions that Natalie loses track of the adjectives already used.

Then, suddenly, they break for lunch. The second inspector gives her a voucher for the cafeteria and points her in the right direction. She wanders there as if in a daze; if it wasn't located in the same place as in her building, she would have probably lost her way. She tries to gather her thoughts as she pokes at the institutional food. The mass of overlapping conspiracy theories is too much for her to untangle; it is just so mind-bogglingly insane. Even if there is some sense hidden in there somewhere, there is no way to recognize it as such. She decides to abandon the goal of getting new information and focus on making sure that she doesn't get so disoriented or worn down that she accidently says "yes" to anything.

She wonders if her conspiracy theories about Marne, the Committee and a sprinkling of anonymous amoebas in key positions sound as insane. She doesn't think that they are insane, since Marne evidently got the information about contaminated water from somewhere and he had to be well connected for Andesmas to accept the invitation. Still, without some distance from the situation, it is difficult to tell. The more she thinks about it, the less sure she is about everything. Unlike in the valley, she never saw anyone or thing sick or dead from typhoid; she has taken André's word for it. Even if she saw the bodies and tests, she wouldn't trust herself to see clearly. She would have had to spend far more than an afternoon reading about the disease; she would have to be familiar with the whole range of possibilities, given the symptoms, and come up with a real diagnosis. And then there is the seafood bit, which she has always had trouble believing.

She reigns in her thoughts as much as she can, all the while resisting the urge to pull out her flask. The more she questions everything, the more vulnerable she is going to be to the questions the investigators will be throwing at her this afternoon. It would be different if it was possible to come to a definitive conclusion, but, without being privy to Committee discussions, having more education and a pile of other things, it was not. She makes an effort to eat what's on her plate and focuses on the similarities between the small boardroom and the interrogation room. They are, after all, practically the same, so this whole experience should be treated as an ordinary meeting, albeit one that is uncomfortably long.

The afternoon session immediately gets into an unsurprising subject, at least in retrospect: her family. They start with the role she played in drafting the charter, how she convinced her parents to sign it and so on. In reality, she knew nothing about the charter and her parents' decision to sign it until after the fact. In her youthful exuberance, she was proud of them taking such a principled stance. She was both scared and excited about what might happen next. She imagined that her parents would go to prison and become high-profile symbols of the fight for change, that she and her sister would galvanize support from the outside and stoke the fires of protest that the charter had sparked.

Instead, nothing happened. The government did send a couple of leaders to prison, but not her parents. The charter sparked nothing; it was limited to an intelligentsia that the general population had little connection to. The back and forth between the two groups reminds her of the conversation between George and Tom; even if the intelligentsia had a point, they had neither the perspective nor the legitimacy to rally people to their banner. Everyone recognized that there were bad things going on and everyone disagreed on whether it was worth risking losing the good things in an effort to change society. People who signed the charter typically did so because they felt that it was their moral responsibility to say something in the face of the Committee's repression, regardless of whether it would inspire others or not. She was at the time of the opinion that it was necessary to go further.

The investigators continue, asking when and where she has seen her family in the years following the charter. Her mother had given up her position as the famous and respected judge Andesmas and his personal amoeba mentioned to work somewhere in the eastern prairies several months before the charter. After, when it was clear that nothing was going to happen, she went back to it. There was really nothing else she could have done. Natalie's sister left home to go to university soon after the charter and found that life was more pleasant with her peers when she distanced herself from her family. Her father wanted to be closer to his wife and thought that she would want to be closer to her mother, so suggested to Natalie that the two of them move out to the main prairie city. Natalie refused, since her life, such as it was, was in the capital. After a great deal of reflection and figuring out logistics for her, who was still a minor at the time, he moved to the prairies alone.

There were some early, abortive attempts to bring the family back together for events and such, mainly spearheaded by her mother. Those faded when her sister told her parents rather directly that seeing them made her life impossible. Her parents assumed that the same was true for her and she did not bother correcting them. So, she has not seen her family in quite some time, since she finished high school. It was hard at first—she took a lot of shifts at the laundry—but she got used to it fairly quickly. When the poetry dropped out of the series of books she was reading at the time, she was convinced that she knew exactly how the author felt.

The interrogation shifts to her dad's old milieu when he lived in the capital. They would chiefly like to know what response she and her co-conspirators are planning for the release of the counter-charter. Her father has been the subject of constant surveillance since before she was born; all his old haunts have the three black cars permanently stationed across the street. She used to pick up laundry at some of them, but hasn't been since. The community was, and undoubtedly still is, one of artists, musicians and other creative types—everything she and her fellow members of the amoeba-ox continuum are not. If she showed up at one of the cafés, the patrons would be liable to scatter like the audience at the puppet show.

Overall, she finds the afternoon questioning far more relaxing than the morning. She has run through that part of her life a million times in her head, examining every detail until it was worn through. Unlike with the outbreak, she has enough information and expertise to have come to reasonable enough conclusions and to have stored the file in her not very well organized mental archives. Yes, she feels abandoned by her family; no, she does not harbor a grudge against them for it. Yes, she still feels guilt for not doing more to see her parents; no, that guilt is not overwhelming or even that important in the grand scheme of things. Yes, she appreciates the difficult choices her parents felt they had to make; yes, that is part of her motivation to avoid situations that require such choices.

As the questions continue, she thinks that she might have been too hasty in putting the amoeba-ox continuum in opposition to creativity. If one was to believe what the investigators were insinuating in their questions, she was in the middle of masterminding the overthrow of the government in a dozen different ways, was central to the smuggling and distribution of underground books for the entire country, had daily coded conversations with her father, was plotting to destroy grain stock and orchestrate a famine, was behind several incidents of student unrest and dissatisfaction at the university, etc., etc. All those fictions must take an enormous amount of imagination, which surely would be appreciated by artists and the like.

The only difficulty she has is with the responses. There is no pithy half-truth that avoids giving the police more than what they started with. She toys with the idea of repeating back the central object of the question, such as "book" and "government," but is not comfortable with what might be read into the words. Despite the disconnect, she continues to use "The Towers is X," cycling through adjectives in an increasingly ordered though no more sensible way. The inspectors record her nonsensical responses without comment and move on. They will frequently repeat questions in slightly different ways, which would likely trip her up if she was trying to keep to a coherent story, but they make no difference under the circumstances. Even without a monotonous "I refuse to testify," the inspectors probably think that she is her father's daughter; perfectly at home in the interrogation room, even if it took her a morning to find her rhythm. They do not bother insisting on more reasonable answers since there is little chance that will work.

Every time she says, "The Towers," it sounds to her more and more like a mantra. The words put her mind at ease and distance her from the room, the questions, her past and everything else that weighs on her. The problem with Andesmas's paradise as far as she is concerned is that society, or some future version of it, is supposed to be there; people will be there Andesmas would reply with impatience that paradise for us is necessarily a human paradise. He would say that conflict is inevitable and ultimately positive so long as society has reached a point where it can be dealt with constructively. She is conflating utopia and a state of static perfec-

tion, which is completely wrong-headed and potentially dangerous. Difference and conflict give paradise color or, to use a musical
metaphor, harmony. Paradise is an orchestra, where instruments
are playing different notes together, notes that are sometimes dis-
cordant yet always resolve into a coherent communal whole. He
would never outright admit, but always imply, that a conductor—
the Committee—is crucial for everyone to come together.

He could very well be right, but Natalie doesn't care. That sort
of paradise holds nothing for her. The Towers as a nuclear explosion, an unknowable purity where the complexities of life don't
apply, is far more appealing. It is a state that doesn't need an explanation to connect this seemingly endless stream of inane accu-
sations and a society of constructive harmony. Perhaps a nuclear
explosion is a bad comparison, given its aftermath of destruction
and, if it's used on a live target, misery. Perhaps a star would be
better, something faraway and brilliant. The details don't matter,
so long as it is an idea foreign to this grey concrete bunker, Albert's
death, Tom's wheezing cough, paradise as clean running water
and everything else that comes with the human context.

The afternoon is over before she knows it.

"Thank you for coming, Ms. Chaulieu," the first inspector says.
"Your cooperation has been invaluable."

"We will make sure to have lemon tea on hand for your next
visit," the second inspector adds, pointing to the still full cup he
brought in the morning.

"Okay," Natalie mumbles, slowly bringing herself back to the
present.

The two inspectors escort her out. By the time they have gone
through the all too familiar building, she has the impulse to go to
the bar. She puts up a token struggle and then heads to the usual
spot. Entering, she sees the typical mid-week crowd at the ordinary table. They shift over to give her room to sit down, as if she
had been in the office with them the whole day, going through red
files and typing up plans.

Chapter 14

"You know that the police have started following me, yes?" Natalie asks.

"Yes," André responds.

"They interrogated me yesterday."

"But it wasn't your first time."

"It was, actually. Why would you assume that it wasn't my first time?"

André shrugs.

"Right. Anyway, I thought that it would be best to let you know, in case there is some extra scrutiny on the project. First the water plant, now this . . ."

"You should add yourself to the list."

"Yeah, you're right. How many times have you been stuck with a Committee liaison on a project?"

"It's rare."

"And you didn't send the police an anonymous tip, just to get me off your back?"

"That would have attracted more unwanted attention to the outbreak."

"So, you thought about it?"

"No."

"They didn't even have lemon tea."

"You didn't ask for fermented blood?"

"Ha! I should have. I didn't even think of it. Next time, though. How did the tests go?"

"We know what we are dealing with, which is good. It won't be an easy clean-up, which will be a challenge."

"What are we dealing with?"

"From the evidence, it looks like the dirt that was in this area was reused when the Towers was developed without much thought for what was in it. There are two problems: first, when this place was a small town, there were a lot of earth closets—dirt outhouses. When they excavated to build the city they just mixed all the dirt into one big pile."

"Including all the excrement."

"Yes. The second problem is that they did not compact the dirt very well—it probably didn't have the composition to be able to be well compacted. So, over the years, with changing humidity and the buildings pressing down, it started heaving."

"Which explains why the roads are all buckled."

"Yes. That ruptured the water pipes, which made things worse. Interestingly, it also managed to insulate the pipes enough so that the pressure held and the water still got through. It is a strange situation but, I am told, not unheard of."

"Does all the dirt have to be removed?"

"That would be the best option. At the very least, the pipes need to be replaced and they need to be insulated and packed with clean fill."

"What about the buildings?"

"They are still shifting, apparently. The foundations are not in good shape. There is a risk that the water connections into the buildings will break once the pipes are replaced. So, optimally, somehow, the buildings would need to be stabilized as well. I don't know if that can be reasonably done."

"That's a lot to take in. What do I put in my report?"

"The basics; focus on the source of the contamination without blaming anyone or suggesting solutions."

"Marne will be happy, now that we are saying that it's the dirt and not the water."

"There might still be questions about why the pipes were installed in unstable soil."

"So, the Committee will want to know more."

"They will. The costs will be too high to be covered by Public Health or the city. Once we have an estimate, which is the next step, we will have to bring it to their attention and see how they want to proceed. You can put that in your report as well."

"I will give them a heads-up, then, so they'll be better prepared when they learn the full extent of the issues."

"If you don't mind."

"Not at all. I'm here to help."

They sit in silence for a moment, Natalie reflecting on what this means for the Towers and André sorting the borehole test results he has laid out on the table.

"It's like Death's revenge," she says. "People pulled down her town and thought they could outsmart her with a city built on technology, chlorine and centrifuges. The cabaret was opened as an homage to a bygone, superstitious era. Anyone who really believed in her coming to town and getting drunk on blood was laughed at. And now we learn that the whole city is built on disease."

He stops sorting the papers and looks at her with slight amusement.

"Human ignorance and stupidity isn't good enough for you?" he asks.

"Those are strong words, coming from you."

He shakes his head and finishes his sorting.

"I don't think the two are incompatible," she says.

"Fair enough."

They leave the cabaret and, after he scans the sky, he turns to her.

"I wouldn't worry about the police," he says. "In my experience, they like to check up on people from time to time. It's like they have a list that they go through from top to bottom and then start at the top again. Every five years or so, they follow me for a week or two, sometimes invite me down for a cup of coffee, and then disappear. Maybe they think it helps keep people in line, maybe it's to keep their files up to date. From what I hear about your parents, I imagine that everyone in your family made the list. I doubt that it has anything to do with the outbreak."

"Well, that's comforting. Thank you."

He nods and walks away. She wanders along the street, looking for a shop that sells blankets. Now that the exact source of the typhoid has been found, she no longer has a work-related reason to come down here. All she has to do now is write her final report and return to the office. Maybe Andesmas will have something else for her to do, another highly sensitive international incident, but she doubts it. She would like to make coming here a habit, though; a way to escape the grey reality of the capital that is a quick metro ride away. The idea that the city is built on a layer of disease is, oddly enough, an added attraction.

It takes her half an hour to find a blanket. She passes the store without noticing the bedding and other household goods in the window. Her eyes are on the street, picking out heaves, cracks and any other sign of the shifting dirt underneath. Where she is, on the main road, there is little indication that anything is amiss. When she almost walks into one of the stopped delivery vehicles, she decides that she can't win; either she focuses on what's above the ground and risks tripping or she focuses on the ground and risks running into things. She nonetheless makes her way to the end of the block without major incident and decides to look back to see if there are any subtle bulges or depressions in the road that are only noticeable when a larger area is in view. She can't tell, however, if the bulges she sees are purposeful, to allow the road to drain, or not. As her interest in the obvious effects of the shifting dirt fades, the display window and her intention to buy a blanket come back to the forefront.

The unevenness of the side streets are as she remembers when she was more taken by the contrast between the grey and white than the quality of the surface. She wonders if George could set up a camera and film one of the streets—preferably a street with large stained-glassed windows on either side to provide extra color—for a month or a year and then cut the film so that it looked like it was writhing. She wonders if the audience would interpret the movement as a reaction to the pain of so much disease just under the skin or as a reflection of the industry of mole-like creatures, who are burrowing and creating homes for their families. Perhaps, they would content themselves with the idea that even what they assume to be the most sturdy and inert of substances—concrete, paving stones and asphalt—are fluid and dynamic over time. Andesmas would love the idea; he would work it into his motivational speeches about the changing nature of utopia.

By the time she arrives at the puppet show, the only place she can think of finding Theo during the day, the puppeteers are finishing off a show. She automatically looks for the red shirt she first saw him in, before switching to his blond hair and general size. The crowd is thin today, so it does not take long for her to conclude that he is not there. She is relieved, as her first conversation with him was awkward enough and she doesn't want him to read too much into the blanket. She leans against the wall halfway down the block and, belatedly, thinks to look back to see if the cop is still following her. He is and, assuming that he is the same amoeba as last time, takes up his usual spot on the corner. The audience is too engrossed by the show to notice. She suspects that they would notice and scatter if he tried to get closer, although she is not sure why the same wouldn't apply to her. The word might have gotten around that she is not a bad sort, but that would imply that they are able to recognize her. Maybe her amoeba suit is not as sure a disguise as she thought; maybe she looks too unhealthy to be a standard issue cog.

She approaches the puppeteers after the show.

"You seem so wholesome out here; putting on puppet shows, surrounded by freshly touched up white walls," Natalie observes.

"You need to stick around and watch more of the shows," the second puppeteer says. "Our sacred national tradition is full of depravity, misery and all that good stuff. Perfect for young, impressionable minds."

"I guess it might entice kids to help make a better world, or at least remind them that the past isn't really a place they would want to be."

"I'm not sure that's what they're getting out of it," the first puppeteer says. "I suppose that one can hope that we're not turning them into a cult of incestuous serial killers."

"What brings you and your grey looking friend to our humble street? Any more word on the outbreak?" the second asks.

Natalie gives them a brief rundown on the progress of the investigation; basically a dry run of the report she is about to write.

"Wow," the first says. "So, there's excrement everywhere? That's really disturbing, all joking aside."

"I guess that explains why it's such a challenge to level the stage," the second adds.

"I imagine that we'll have to move the show, if they have to dig it all up."

"You could always go on the road," Natalie suggests. "I ran into someone in a village about an hour out of town who went on endlessly about the wonderful times he had as a kid whenever a travelling puppet show came through. It was apparently quite the tradition, but isn't done so much anymore. Right up your alley, so to speak."

"That's an interesting idea," the first says.

"Expensive," The second adds.

"Maybe we can get a grant through the school."

The two immediately get into the options and logistics. Natalie starts imagining killing three birds with one stone. If a puppet show did go through the village, George could shoot a film on it. It would be a feel good story about life in the village that wouldn't have to be doctored; a story he could feel proud of. Then he could give a copy to Tom, who had his heart set on seeing the positive side of his village onscreen. Tom would be doubly happy, since the travelling puppet show alone would be a dream come true. Then she starts to think about the details; all the dead livestock would have to be taken care of, as well as the other traces of the fog. The girls would have to be warned about the respiratory problems so that they wouldn't be unnerved by the coughing and wheezing and run a piece that would stand up despite the regular interruptions. Even then, they would be breathing in the chemicals when they were there. It probably wouldn't matter, so long as they didn't stay long, but the thought of it is still off-putting.

Her thoughts go further, following those she had in the apartment of Albert's family. Once Death is drunk enough, any fermented blood will do. At the beginning, though, she has a certain level of discernment. Albert's fresh blood would have been just what she needed to stomach the harsh fluid that ran in the veins of Natalie and André. Natalie could see Death settling down in the Two Caskets—the village only being built after the first major plague—and drinking her way through the two puppeteers before settling on the carcinogen-laden brew from the villagers. She would meticulously arrange the progression and end with the longest-serving factory worker, an ox with so much heavy metal in him that if he were melted down, he would make a perfectly respectable ingot.

The train of thought makes Natalie terribly thirsty. She glances back to see the mass of grey still on the corner and makes the effort to resist. After she has finished with the puppeteers, she can duck around the corner and drink in relative privacy.

"Anyway," Natalie says, interrupting the puppeteers, "I actually didn't come to chat or give you the news, though both are worthwhile. I was hoping to run into Theo."

"He has been coming less and less during the week," the first says. "I think that he is back at school. I did suggest it a couple of times, very lightly. We don't really want him to become a serial killer."

"We reminded him too much of Albert," the second adds, "and without Albert's overactive imagination, it was never the same. He never really found what he was looking for."

"It's sad, though, to see that connection fade away. It is for the best; his mother must have been worried sick. It's for the best."

"He still comes around on weekends though, and sometimes after school. We suggested that he bring his mother, but he never has. You can come around then."

"Now that the investigation has run its course," Natalie says, "I'm not going to be around much. Could you just give him this, the next time you see him?"

Natalie hands the blanket to the first puppeteer.

"For him to sit on," Natalie explains, "when he comes again. I noticed that most people in the crowd had one."

"That's really thoughtful of you," the first says. "We will of course give it to him."

"Don't read too much into it," Natalie says. "I just had it on my list of things to do. I don't recall why it was there, but it was. So, here we are."

"I'm sure that Theo will minimize its importance, as well," the second points out.

Natalie starts to walk away, past the puppeteers. She stops and turns back after a couple of steps.

"We will probably see each other again at the cabaret, though," Natalie suggests. "Assuming of course that your being there wasn't a one off thing."

"We're there fairly often," the second says, "at least compared to some people. If the roads get dug up, that's another story. And now that you've put the idea of a road trip out there . . ."

The first nods in agreement.

"It's a nice place," Natalie continues. "It has the otherworldly atmosphere of the Towers without the austere whiteness. An agreeable break from the capital, and I don't get the impression that I'm going to sully up the place just by being around."

She immediately wonders why she felt the need to say the last part. In order to avoid blurting out anything else that might come to mind, she turns and quickly walks around the corner. She keeps going, pulling her flask out for a quick drink without slowing down. A moment later, she trips and lands on her knees. After taking the requisite time to curse, she rises and keeps going. It is just as well that she rarely had to come through here when she worked for the laundry, though having a bag stuffed with linens would have made for a more pleasant fall. Maybe she should have bought a pillow along with the blanket, even if it wasn't on her list. Unrelatedly, it would be great to find a hiding spot where she could watch how well the amoeba trailing after her navigated the uneven pavement.

Her thoughts never rise above pettiness and she is just as happy to leave them there for the time being. André could be right about the police presence being routine and temporary, but, when she runs through the possibilities, she can't help believing that there's more to it. Perhaps it's just a question of her family haunting her despite her distance from them; even if the police sometimes blended into the background when she was growing up, they were never completely absent. Now that they are back, it's difficult to imagine that they will ever really go away. Given all that, she is better off not thinking about it, if she can manage to distract herself with whatever happens to pique her interest and slow everything down with a drink or two.

Chapter 15

The apartment is starting to get cluttered with everything but still edible food. Natalie reflects on the tension between who she is and her decidedly superficial and convenient notion of domestic paradise. A spotless apartment is an aberration; a temporary state that is constantly pulled toward disorder—or chaos, if she is aiming for the dramatic. There might be a point when George will become native to the environment, when he will no longer have to impose his will on the uncooperative— or hostile—objects that surround him. The relationship might become symbiotic, mutually supportive, or something along those lines. Then maybe she wouldn't see the clutter as normal. If everyone in the country is like her, Andesmas will have his work cut out for him.

She hears a knock on the door. Her thoughts immediately go to the police; another interrogation or maybe, for variety, a search. At least George imposes his will with a vacuum and healthy food. This whole push for societal harmony is far too forceful and vio-lent for her taste, even if almost all the violence is implied rather than real. She is slow to get up from the couch, expecting them to kick down the door any moment now. Nothing happens by the time she reaches the door. She pauses, contemplates going back to the couch without checking to see if anyone is still in the hallway. Not wanting to deal with a broken door and figuring that there are few questions left to ask, she opens it.

George is waiting patiently, a paper bag in his hand.

"You have a key," Natalie points out as she heads back to the couch. "You could have let yourself in and saved me the trouble."

"We haven't seen each other since the road trip; I didn't want to assume."

He goes into the kitchen and puts the bag in the fridge. Then he leans against the doorframe between the kitchen and living room.

"How have you been?" he asks.

"Well enough, nothing to complain about. You?"

"Better. Thanks for giving me some time."

"I was the one who gave you the ultimatum."

"True, but it was the right thing to do. Hanging around feeling sorry for myself and expecting you to put up with it was not fair on you."

"Okay, so you've come back. What now?"

"I haven't really come back. One of the reasons I didn't feel comfortable using the key, actually."

"So, you've come back to say that you aren't coming back."

"I wanted to explain. I need to explain."

"Okay."

"Do you want something to eat? I brought food."

"Of course you did. No; just say what you have to say."

"Well, at least let me make some tea."

"Not in the mood for whisky, this time?"

"That was a mistake."

He goes into the kitchen and puts the kettle on the stove. When he doesn't immediately come back, she sighs and follows him. She finds him leaning on the counter. She bites back a comment and counts to ten as she washes a pair of cups in the sink. She puts them on the counter and drops a teabag from a tin in each. Then she sits at the table. The two wait for the water to boil in silence. When the water is ready, he pours the cups and brings them to the table, sitting down opposite her. She starts to swirl the teabag around the cup.

"A mistake," she prompts.

"It just made things worse."

"It helped you come up with the idea to go out to the village. It was perhaps not the most effective means, but it worked."

"That had more to do with you dragging me to the cabaret; I needed the air, to be distracted."

She continues to swirl the teabag.

"Going to the village was necessary. It was the last straw; I can't help people like that. Even if I were a genius with complete creative freedom, nothing that I could create would have changed anything. It would just be the same arguments repeated in another way, to be brushed off as if they were completely insubstantial. And that's fine, I accept it. More importantly, I am no longer doing something where my uselessness is thrown in my face every day."

"You have a new job?"

"Yes, I have a new job."

"What is it?"

"Another documentary, but one where I don't have to shoehorn reality into whatever neat little message the Committee wants to send out into the world."

"Specifically?"

"Our classical marionette tradition and how it is being kept alive at The National School of Puppetry."

"Ha! It's a small world. Tonda Keller, I suppose?"

"He is at the center of it, yes. I didn't know you knew Tonda Keller."

"I've never met the man, but have run into a couple of his students in the Towers. At the cabaret, the two women I was with at the booth."

"I don't really recall."

"Your mind was elsewhere, I understand; happens to me too. Anyway, they run a more or less traditional street puppet show. After the mayor's trip down memory lane when we were at the village, I have been thinking about travelling puppet shows. I mentioned the idea to them and they might just do it."

"That's nice, he'll enjoy it."

"That would give you the opportunity to film it; a happy documentary about the revival of this old tradition, showing the village in an idyllic light."

"You didn't suggest that to them, did you?"

"No, it just crossed my mind."

"Because that is a terrible idea. I mean, haven't you been listening to me? I would still have to shoot a bunch of people who have managed to convince themselves that ingesting sulfur dioxide and the devil knows what else is somehow necessary to live a good life. I would still have to edit out all the coughing fits from the interviews I would need to do. The performance would be a sad spectacle, a minor distraction from the chemicals eating away at them."

"Fair enough. It was a bad idea."

"Sorry, I went too far."

"You are passionate about it."

"That's just it; I can't not care. I tried, but it's not possible for me. I can't be like you, no matter how much easier my life would be if that were the case."

"Okay."

"Your puppeteers might even be traumatized by the experience, if they see the dead zone, for instance."

"I figure they can handle it, but you could be right."

"All I can do is lose myself in fulfilling work, where I can make a difference. It can be the smallest thing; I don't have any pretentions of changing the world. Just something. With Keller, maybe I can bring marionettes to a whole new audience. This is a tradition we can be proud of, and I can communicate that. I might even be instrumental in giving the form international exposure. The Committee wants to increase promotion of the country and, if my film is good enough, it could be on the front lines. Then maybe they will entrust me with other high-profile work, far from the obscure corners of everyday life."

"The dark side of progress."

"I don't know if I would call that progress, but yes."

"The main difference between now and the misery of the nineteenth century is that we are better at sweeping the problems under the rug."

"Right. And if I was in the position to expose the misery, if I had the courage to go it alone when I can't even convince sick people that they are dying . . ."

"Keller is a good model for you. He's not out there saving lives or risking his own. Nothing he does will revolutionize anything. Yet, nobody denies that what he does is important. Keeping the nation's culture alive is significant."

"That's exactly what I think. I mean, I know that the Committee is selective about what culture is worth preserving and I don't always agree with them. Your father's books, for example."

"Keller's work, if it's anything like that of his students, is worth promoting. My dad and the Committee don't change that."

"I still feel that I am trying to convince myself that I'm not doing something wrong. I can't help being suspicious of every assignment the government gives me."

"Well, if you came back to say that you are not coming back, you won't have me to assuage your doubts."

"Yes, you're right. This is selfish of me. If you want me to go, I'll go."

She shrugs and finally takes a sip of her tea. The last time she was sitting at a kitchen table having a discussion like this, it was her father opposite her. They were mirror images of each other; swirling the bags of lemon tea in their cups for longer than was reasonable, the thoughts in their heads circling at the same speed. The difference was that his ideas generally ended in action, even if it was only putting them on paper in the journal he edited. It was like the two of them were centrifuges in the water plant, only someone forgot to put the chemical in her mind. His thoughts came out clean and well organized while hers were just as messy and unpalatable as they had been before being run through the process. She doesn't imagine that such thoughts are actually a vector for disease, though the Committee would likely disagree. She decides to give up on the tea and brings a bottle and two glasses to the table. There was enough familial nostalgia to last a year at the police station.

"You should defect," Natalie says.

"What?"

"You should find a way to leave the country."

"I have thought about it. We all have at one time or another, I suppose. My place is here, though. Unlike you, I actually like being close to my family."

"Are they happy?"

"More or less."

"Do you add to their happiness, when they are? Or do you spread your unhappiness? Can you leave the dead zone around the factories behind when you're with them or do you act the same way as when you're here?"

Natalie pours a glass for herself. George covers his glass before she can do the same for him.

"That's just simplistic," George replies. "We all support each other; we are there for each other through thick and thin. I try not to burden them, it's true, but I don't really hide anything either. We have issues, but we are committed to working through them and sticking together."

"But you are giving up on us? Not that I think you should do anything different, you understand."

"There is no give-and-take with you. Your advice has pretty consistently been that I should care less than I do. No one in my family would suggest that. And then there is the means you use for yourself to be numb to the world."

He gestures at the bottle.

"I had a moment of weakness after the film got cancelled," he continues. "I wanted to get away from my frustration and guilt the easiest way possible. You helped me see that it wasn't the answer. Yet here you are, not wanting to deal with what I am saying. You use your flask as a barrier against the world. I would love to be able to support you; I would love to feel that I am contributing more to us than cooking and cleaning."

She takes a drink and begins to wonder what food he brought.

"It's not just that you don't care, though. Sometimes you have the most brilliant flashes of imagination, and I just can't follow. I am supposed to be a talented artist; I have a shelf full of awards and my mother keeps a scrapbook of glowing reviews that are trying to convince me of it. For almost all the time I have known you, you have worked in a drab office doing the devil knows what; some sort of drudgery that probably leaves you deader inside than the alcohol does. How can I support you if I can't keep up?"

She thinks of Keller's file, undoubtedly still sitting in the middle of her desk at work. The essence of relative genius biding its time in the bunker. "Relative genius" seems to her suddenly an odd expression, as if "genius" is not a word that can be qualified. In any case, George has dipped into melodrama. She can tell him to leave at any time, but she doesn't. On some level, she probably wants to prolong the scene and delay the inevitable. On another, the more he goes on, the less sympathetic he is to her and the easier it will be to deprive herself of this invading force for domestic utopia.

"Who am I to know, right?" George continues. "I care deeply for you and that blinds me. I see such potential, but maybe it's simply that I want so much more for you. I hope that you decide to move beyond your indifference, to not let your aversion to unhappiness or joy stop you from seeing where those moments of brilliance can lead."

"That's a bit melodramatic, don't you think?"

"Yeah, and you've already dismissed it."

"True. You're treating me like one of your poor village folk who should be doing so much more for themselves, if only they weren't so deluded."

"You're right, sort of. But you aren't so deluded; otherwise, you wouldn't drink so much. I know that I'm being an idiot; I just don't want to leave without telling you this."

"You need to leave the country."

Natalie empties her glass and pours another.

"You mentioned that."

"People everywhere might be like they are here, but they might not be. If you stay, you are just going to run into self-destructive sorts incapable of realizing anything interesting. And the occasional hippo. Elsewhere at least there's a possibility of finding people who are either like you or at least are more grateful for your pathological need to fix everyone."

"I don't think I've tried to fix you."

"You even tried to fix my apartment."

"If anything, I've tried to be more like you. I actually thought that caring less was the answer."

"It was. And I predict that you'll be bitching and moaning to your adoring mother—how many times has she waxed on about your flashes of brilliance, reflected for the world to see on the big screen?—when you find out that Keller is not the deity you are building him up to be. You'll cajole him to do more to convince the Committee that all culture is important and that banning whatever they find objectionable is not right. You might even bring up my dad's books, out of a lingering sense of attachment to me. When he refuses, your world will crumble once more."

"I don't think that's fair."

"Wait, so this isn't the time to say what should be said before you take your leave?"

"It's not the time to lash out."

"You are like a parent who is living through his children. You have accepted your own mediocrity, but feel that if you can just convince someone else to do something more, you can revel in the reflection of their glory. Had the villagers fought for better filters, you would be patting yourself on the back for all the great work you did. If I go on to do something amazing, you'll congratulate yourself for laying it all out here and now, and persuading me that I am actually capable of doing great things."

"You're right; you should get whatever you need to off your chest now. And you should drink another glass or three and do whatever helps you get through this."

"And now you're a martyr. You'll sit there passively and take all the barbs I throw at you because you care enough about me. Truly, you are a mensch."

He refills her glass without comment.

"I bet you're convinced that if the Keller film goes well and you are able follow it with a string of higher profile work, you will unabashedly promote your vision of the world to the Committee. When the time is right, you will stop trying to work through others and stand up for all the delusional little people who don't know any better. You will make sure the filters are installed and that books are not banned. Only, you won't. Either you'll manage to become a member of the Committee, at which point you will simply impose your vision, believing in your heart of hearts that you know best or the risk of losing your guild membership and falling from your vaunted position as premier auteur of the land will stop you from giving your opinion on anything at all."

"It's nice to know that you have such a high opinion of me."

"Isn't it, though? I remember clearly when we skulked at the edge of the main square in the Towers and you admitted what you considered to be a cowardly fear of losing your membership. All I'm doing is extrapolating from what you have confessed to me. This is the opinion you have of yourself, when you are honest about it."

"Perhaps that is the main difference between us; I believe that I can change and do better and you assume everything stays the same. It would be less sad if you didn't wake up every morning, put on your grey uniform and join thousands of others who do exactly the same thing."

"Sounds like paradise to me."

"Yeah. I'm done, I have nothing else to say. You?"

She shakes her head. She is tempted to ask him to stay and clean the apartment one last time, but decides that it is better to leave it in its natural state. He gets up and goes to the door. She stays in the kitchen. She hears the door open, and then some parting words.

"I wish you all the best. Remember the food in the fridge."

She hears the sound of the door close. She pours a token amount into the second glass and, imagining that her father is across from her, toasts and empties her glass.

Chapter 16

The only flash of brilliance that Natalie sees is the main square of the Towers, getting in the way of the analysis of a new red file. On the one hand, she would prefer that the pages were surfaces alive with energy, as if freshly painted over and already concentrating the heat and light of the day. Then she wouldn't have to read the particulars of people's lives and determine how they should be handled. On the other hand, not only would it be annoyingly bright and reveal aspects of the drab office that she would prefer stay hidden, it would soon be mind-numbingly boring. She prefers that the edge be taken off her thoughts and the input from the world around her; a blank surface would be going too far. The brilliance of the Towers only works for her in contrast to the eclecticism of the capital, the tourist-like blobs and a thousand other details. Wiping out the words of a file erases the entire distilled world contained within.

When Natalie resumed her ordinary office life, she spent an hour staring at the Keller file, still exactly where she had left it in the middle of her desk. The file's world had been corrupted by her interactions with the puppeteers and Theo, as well as by George's new assignment. It was no longer a self-contained whole that she could grasp and judge; she had become aware of all the gaps and knew that the answers could only be found in the outside world. Seeking answers would set a dangerous precedent, putting in motion a train of thought that could only end in connecting the files to living, breathing people. That would be a needless complication that had no place in the central bureaucracy. She eventually put it at the bottom of the incoming pile and pulled an anonymous file from the top.

A week passes, the red files cross her desk at a steady, unhurried cadence. When she has a flash of brilliance, she lets it run its course. While she prefers reviewing the files to be uncomplicated, regular reminders that she herself is not is not unwelcome. The flashes stop her from getting pulled too far into the life stories, so she is less exhausted when the plans are finished. Thankfully, as far as she is concerned, they also slow her progress in reading through them, leaving her level of efficiency untouched. It would be disturbing to discover that her time in the Towers has made her a better worker. After a couple of files, she still feels the need to get out of the bunker and take a sip from her flask. She is in the middle of getting up when she sees Andesmas's amoeba approaching. She sits back down and waits for him to cross the office, a vague feeling of déjà-vu tickling the back of her mind.

Once he reaches her desk, they head to the small boardroom without a word. She starts to wonder what sort of assignment she could get that would be more absurd than the international seafood crisis.

"Andesmas must not like you much," Natalie says as they sit down across from each other. "Putting you in an interrogation room with me a third time must be a special sort of torture for you."

"This isn't an interrogation room."

"Are you sure about that?"

"Mr. Andesmas feels that it is important to let you know what decisions have been made in regard to the outbreak."

"Now you are just trying to change the subject."

"I am trying to get to the point."

"Are you behind the police surveillance?"

"What?"

"You said that there would be repercussions for the apparent lack of respect I have shown you. Are you behind the surveillance?"

"I am not behind anything of the sort. I don't know what you are talking about."

"This whole interrogation thing is new to me. Let me go again: why have you been undermining the Committee by obstructing the investigation of one their agents?"

"You're insufferable."

"Please answer the question."

"Please stop playing this childish game."

"So, you consider responding for impeding a Committee project a childish game?"

"I am supposed to say that your reports were very useful to the Committee and . . ."

"Why did you compromise the government by leaking the second report to a third party?"

"Where are you getting this from? What third party?"

"Answering questions with questions does not help your case."

"And what you are doing? I did put in a request for you to go through further training and then be stationed far from any sensitive information. Is that what you want to hear? I'll freely admit it; you have no sense of decency or professionalism. This is a farce, what you are doing; a bad joke that needs to stop, regardless of how convinced Mr. Andesmas is of your good qualities.

"But, you know what? The request was conveniently lost. I put in another, and that was lost too. I don't know who is pulling the strings; I looked through your files, those of your family as well, and nothing came up. You shouldn't be here, with what your parents did. Your sister should not have been able to go to university. Your parents betrayed the Committee—they betrayed our whole society—by signing the charter. And nobody seems to realize that you are just like them, a ticking time bomb that won't be happy until the whole country descends into anarchy.

"Yet, we are here once again. I get to be tortured by you, as you say, and can't do anything about it. The new charter is out and . . ."

"Wait, the counter-charter is out?"

"Don't interrupt me! And it was a huge undertaking. Resources that could have gone toward making this country a better place for everyone were wasted cleaning up the mess that people like your parents made. It is obvious that you are following the same path and that it is only a matter of time before we are going to have to clean up after whatever selfish scheme you come up with. At least your mother made major contributions to our society before your father dragged her down. You aren't even going to have the good grace to do that."

Natalie is too distracted by the news about the new charter for the quip about her mother to fully register.

"If the counter-charter is out," she asks, "what are we all still doing here analyzing red files?"

"That is not what I am here to talk about."

"They must be finding the plans useful; quick guides on how to manipulate people. If they work for pushing people to sign the counter-charter—and, if it's out in the world, they obviously worked—why not use them for every other Committee priority?"

"The Committee found your reports very helpful."

"It won't change much; the pressure points are usually pretty obvious. My sister and I for my parents; hanging our futures on their present actions. But, in case they need something more subtle, the plans could be of some use."

"The threat of destroying your lives didn't seem to faze your parents. Of course, maybe they knew all along that you would be protected."

"You're wrong." Her parents believed by the time they signed that not fighting against systemic repression would be far worse for their daughters in the long run than bending to the threats, regardless of the real consequences.

"On which point?"

She doesn't respond, busy working through what the counter-charter being out in the world really means. The exercise is futile without the text in front of her and knowing who ended up signing it. The first charter was largely symbolic, so she believes that she is on solid ground in considering the new charter the same way. Overall, nothing will change, life will go on. It will dilute the influence of the original and lessen whatever impact it might have had but, the more she thinks about it, the less that matters. Her parents signed it and then went on with their lives; even without the counter-charter taking the spotlight, it was going to fade away.

"Had I known that the news of the charter was going to topple you from your pedestal, I would have mentioned it from the get-go. As I was saying, Mr. Andesmas asked me to relay the decisions made about the outbreak."

Her imagination leads her inexorably back to the Towers. The charter may have inspired her parents, but it is little more to her than another story; a fantasy of human rights and inalienable liberties. There is little original in it—that was never the intent. Even so, the city and the document are not so different. Without the constant attention, the brilliant white fades to grey. The discoloration is only accelerated by the presence of people, of the insalubrity of their daily lives. It is sufficiently challenging to keep a city's worth of surfaces clean enough to reflect certain ideals—even with the government-hired painters roaming the streets. Keeping the ideals written on a piece of paper brilliant over time for an entire society when the government is constantly working to darken them, that seems to her practically impossible.

Maybe her parents knew that the task was beyond them and didn't think it worth trying. It seems counter-intuitive, since that essentially meant that after their symbolic gesture, they gave up fighting—they were no longer models for their children. Whatever; there is always a line. They could have also self-immolated in protest—a sad and tragic flash of brilliance, if there ever was one—but she is just as happy that they didn't. It's just that she can't imagine someone like Andesmas putting on their special suit and using the charter to stir up sentiments of justice and all the rest. The Towers, despite its shaky foundations and fundamental hostility to life, still has the potential to motivate people— even the most insipid of amoebas and plodding of oxen—to work toward some notion of a better world. Sure, even the majority of residents of the capital don't have any idea that the city is right next door, but the possibility is there.

"The first decision," Andesmas's amoeba continues, "is to focus on the initial source of the disease in all internal and external communications. The source is the dirt under the Towers. The dirt contains material from the village's earth closets. Once that is dealt with, the issue will be resolved. 'Water' is to be avoided as it confuses the issue, giving the impression that the source is the water treatment plant or the river, and causes concern that the area of potential outbreak is larger than it is."

"The influence of Hervé Marne, I assume."

"It is a Committee decision. I am sure that they discussed the matter with the experts in the field, including Mr. Marne, and duly reflected on the options. Unlike certain people, they are not inclined to say whatever might come into their minds at a given moment. Do you have an issue with it?"

"Not the decision, no. It seems reasonable enough."

"I'm shocked."

"Me, too."

She holds back getting into her concerns about the process, the leaked report and Marne's political ties. She is fairly sure that this is not the sort of amoeba to leak a report, nor is he in the position to do something constructive about the cozy and politically expedient relations that are baked into the system. He would shrug off any hint of impropriety of his highers and betters, while holding people like her to an impossible standard. In a society whose greatest ambition is to achieve a grey, middling sort of utopia, he is about as idealistic an amoeba as one is likely to run across.

"The next decision is that the Towers is going to be classed as a slum."

"A slum? That seems like overkill. Aren't slums essentially shantytowns, without services or paved roads or anything?"

"It is a technical term, as I understand."

"A technical term that means what exactly?"

"Mainly what you described; serious issues or lack of services, regulation, security and . . . I can't think of any more."

"And you think that the Towers is that far gone?"

"The Committee decided that it was merited. You have an issue with it, though."

"I don't know enough about what the implications are. Maybe it's a good thing, if there is direction that says that improvements to slums should be a priority. Maybe it's bad, if slums are swept under the rug. How am I to know?"

"You can trust that the Committee is doing the right thing."

"Why would I do that?"

"Because you aren't living on the street starving to death."

"That's a pretty low bar."

"You can safely walk down the street at night, you are free to marry whomever you like, you can have a rewarding career; the list is endless."

"That's pretty deluded and hypocritical. Didn't you just say that my sister shouldn't have been able to go to university because of something her parents did? Do you have any idea what was done to people so they would sign the counter-charter? Do you realize that the Committee is killing people in unsafe factories in the name of progress? Wait, don't bother answering; there's no point. So the Towers is now a slum. Great. Are we done?"

She thinks in retrospect that she should have counted to ten before replying.

"The Committee made it known that they are appreciative of the timely and informative reports that were presented to them. In the end, we will have avoided an international incident and will improve the lives of a significant number of people. It has been a group effort and, whether you admit it or not, you have been an integral part in making that happen."

"Now are we done?"

"Thankfully for both of us; yes."

He gets up and leaves without ceremony. She stays in the room for a quick drink before heading back to her desk. Once she is back in her usual spot, she takes a folder from the top of the pile and places it in front of her, unopened. Her thoughts are occupied with imagining the implications of the Towers being a slum, but they get no traction. The image of the brilliant city with an undercurrent of death persists unchanged. She finally resolves to add a visit to the cabaret to talk to André to her mental list, assuming that he still uses it as his office.

After that, her mind immediately jumps to the counter-charter. She fares little better with it, ultimately finding no reason to consider it any differently from the original. It gives the government something to point to, if anyone has the temerity to use the original to criticize them, but it would never be used as a vision to which the whole country can rally. She wonders how much leverage had to be used to get the appropriate people to sign it; another detail she will likely never know. At least Keller was not among them.

Her usual work rhythm then imposes itself once more; she opens the folder and methodically goes though the abstracted elements of someone's life. After work, she goes to the usual bar for the usual amount of time, and then she heads home to her comforting clutter.

She is sitting on the couch, thinking about nothing much at all, when there is a knock on the door. She idly considers answering it but decides that it isn't worth the effort. Another knock follows, accompanied by another sprinkling of idle thought. Then, a couple of minutes later, she hears a piece of paper being slid under the door. The thought of paper brings her mind back to the charters, which is to say that nothing good can come of it. Nonetheless, when she has to leave the couch anyway to go to the bathroom, she takes the long route back and picks it up.

It is a short note from George. He says that a piece of Keller's has been accepted at a festival in the west. He convinced the government that filming an international audience's enthusiastic response to a performance of a cultural masterpiece by one of the country's leading artists was an opportunity that couldn't be missed. So, he would be going too. He just wanted to say that he had thought a lot about what she had suggested for his future and that, if the opportunity presented itself, he would do exactly that.

It amuses her that, after all his talk of being close to his family, he is ready to leave them behind. She genuinely believes that he will be better off, settled in another country, especially if the people of that country are more open to his brand of sentimental, paternalistic pseudo-altruism. She might have even inadvertently allowed for the opportunity by putting off submitting the Keller file. At the end of the day, though, she will never really know and it doesn't matter overly much.

Chapter 17

André and Helen are at the usual table, deep in discussion. Natalie orders her lemon tea and joins them. As soon as she sits down, the conversation ceases.

"I think it's time for my first consultation," Helen says, rising.

She is clearly holding back something, which Natalie suspects is a repeat of the observation made the first time the two met. She probably looks unhealthier than ever, what with George's influence fading and her office habits coming back into full force. She feels buoyed by the concentrated energy of the Towers, but, without accoutrements like Andesmas's suit or hair gel, she doesn't exactly project the feeling. Helen's judgmental eye is quickly gone, though, and Natalie settles into swirling her teabag.

"I was wondering if you'd still be around," she says. "The reports are in, the Committee has made its decision; there isn't much left to do."

"True. I'm surprised you are here for the same reason."

"I should be at the office, I guess."

"What brings you back?"

"I don't really understand what it means for the Towers to be classified as a slum."

"They told you what the decision was, then."

"Yeah. Why, didn't they tell you?"

"Not directly, nothing official."

"Do you know what it signifies?"

"That they're going to tear everything down."

"You're being serious? That's completely insane."

"Why?"

"It's not a slum, not really; it's not a collection of shelters slapped together with whatever is at hand on whatever land is available. There are paved roads, sewers, electricity and everything else. "

"The roads are buckling, though. With the fill shifting, a sewer line break is all but inevitable, which will lead to further public health problems. The buildings, as permanent and well thought out as they seem, were shoddily built and their foundations are crumbling. The constant painting has covered up the visible cracks in the walls, but they are there. While the Towers may not obviously be a slum, I don't think that it is unreasonable to classify it as one."

"But people live here."

"As they do in slums. From a public health perspective, it would be better for residents to be rehoused in clean and safe conditions than to turn a blind eye and wait for the city to fall apart."

"And the value, the city is such an important symbol."

"To whom? Practically nobody knows that it exists."

"To at least one member of the Committee."

"I guess the others didn't feel the same way. The city predates the Committee, so they probably don't have a strong attachment to it."

"Yet they promote all sorts of culture that predates them."

"That's different and I think you know it."

She looks down to see that she is spilling tea on the table with her frenetic swirling. She has to make a conscious effort to slow down to her usual pace. She does know it, but she wants to hear someone else say it so that it is not just another thought rattling around in her head.

"I'm not sure that I do know it."

André hesitates before responding.

"The Towers was built before the Committee was in power, when the country was a burgeoning democracy. It is mainly viewed as a successful workers city, a symbol of what society can accomplish cooperatively. The problem is that it is also a reminder that the coercion and repression of the Committee are not necessary to achieve that sort of project. The Committee could even be seen as a hindrance by some people. Your parents, for instance.

"The Committee promotes, or simply tolerates, culture that

does not challenge them. The Death myth associated with the cabaret, for example, isn't a problem. Even the Towers was benign until the outbreak. But now that they actually have to spend a significant amount of money to do something with it, it's not surprising that the choice is to raze everything and start over rather than fixing it up."

"It is just a convenient excuse for them; the city is not safe, so the best they can do is to start over with what they will liberally portray as stronger foundations. I can already see the propaganda reel."

"Regardless of the politics, it is a legitimate choice. The crews can't just go in, dig up the roads, remove the soil and compromised pipes, bring in clean fill and rebuild the roads. They would have to reinforce the foundations of every building in the vicinity or somehow do their work without shaking anything. In addition, more costs will crop up once the structural assessments are done and when they find other issues as they are going along. It would be different if they were only cleaning up a small pocket of contaminated dirt; they really do have to deal with the foundations."

"We will likely never know the real reasons. That doesn't make it any easier to take."

"The other aspect is that the Towers no longer functions as it was intended. We talked about the consequences of industry being moved out. Even if it was a workers utopia at one point, it isn't now."

"You've been around long enough to watch it change, I suppose."

He nods, hesitates and then explains.

"I used to be a specialist in air pollution, back when air pollution was simple. All we had then was the Ringelmann Scale, which measured the darkness of the smoke and how long its trail was from the stack. We just had a piece of paper with gradients of grey on one side and lengths on the other. I went around and visually checked all the stacks. If the smoke exceeded the criteria, I was able to go in then and there and fine the owner or shut down the factory."

"Is everything all right? I've never seen you wax nostalgic before."

"The outbreak was my last file. I am leaving the service."

"Okay, well, congratulations, I guess?"

"Yes, congratulations. Technology has passed me by, now everything has to go through the lab. It's just no longer for me and now I'm old enough to no longer have to do it."

"Is that why you keep looking up at the sky?"

He nods. "Old habit."

"What about nighttime?"

"Sometimes they polluted more at night. It wasn't generally profitable to not work at full capacity during the day, so most were good at following the rules. Occasionally, we would get an owner who would use a furnace, or whatever, that was supposed to have been retired at night. The problem for them was that the process was also less efficient, so, as better techniques brought the prices down, that became less and less cost-effective. Still, if they continued, they usually got away with it. The new style of testing is better on that front."

"But the enforcement isn't. I get the impression that industrial health and safety concerns are being pushed aside in the name of progress."

"There is certainly a conflict between the two."

"If Death were around now, I figure that she would have followed industry when they moved it out of town. The outbreak was a blip, wars are a distant memory . . ."

"Yet the idea remains. There will be another cabaret, likely in this very spot, in whatever development replaces the Towers."

"In a development without poetry, at least not for me."

Now she has almost stopped swirling the bag. She takes a sip and gazes at the coffee line.

"You're right," she continues. "The Towers I want to save is not the city that is right in front of me. The people who live here now are part of the amoeba-ox continuum; there is no community to paint the walls or fill the central square. Without the smoke, the central square is unbearable anyway. I keep chasing this odd, shifting dream; an apocalyptic utopia or a museum piece, depending on the day. It doesn't make sense."

"I can't help you there."

"How is it any different than people in a village who all work in the factories going on about how the factories saved their idyllic home, blind to the fact that they changed everything? It is different though; it's worse. The villagers have the fact that they have lived their entire lives in the village to justify their attachment. A year ago I was just like all the other residents of the capital, barely aware that this place existed. My attachment goes hardly deeper than the last coat of paint.

"I'm not even the sort of worker that would have called this place home when it was everything it was supposed to be. No one in my family is."

"It was a fully functioning city, almost entirely independent from the capital. There weren't just factory workers."

"Yes, I veer from one caricature to another, which just makes everything more pathetic."

She wonders if it is possible that she is just like George. Instead of wanting to save a bunch of people against their will, she wants to save some symbolic version of a city. In her mind, she underlines the word pathetic several times. If the city is crumbling, if it is shot through with death, then so be it. If she loses the main source of poetry in her life, well, it wouldn't be the first time and she can live just as well without it. Whining about it is not helping anyone.

"I like the idea of another incarnation of the cabaret being part of the new development," she says. "Regardless of what it ends up being; giant blocks housing the largest number of people possible or a chic neighborhood of mansions on an artificial hill; the cabaret will keep it all grounded."

"So long as it isn't grim."

"Yeah, this place has a great balance. The first time I was in here, I thought that this is the last drinking hole Death would want to come to get drunk out of her mind. Now I know better; Death is indiscriminating. They don't just serve fermented blood, though. The atmosphere invites you to think about death for a moment, but not to obsess about it. We'll have to suggest that to whoever designs the next version.

"While we're at it, we should demand that next version of the Towers keeps some of the stained glass. Maybe they can add some dedicated puppetry space as well, although formalizing that might make it go stale. They should add more trees in the new square, even if that blocks the view of whatever monumental building ends up in the center."

"There are lots of possibilities when one starts fresh."

"Exactly, and, under the circumstances, there is no point assuming that the Committee will do a bad job with it."

"A boring job, perhaps."

"Yes, but one less likely to be prone to typhoid outbreaks. And it's hard to argue that roving crews of painters are the best use of resources."

"The Committee could redeploy them in the capital."

"But the graffiti artists and taggers do such a good job at keeping the capital interesting, and at a fraction of the price."

"If you like that sort of thing, I guess."

"Chances are that nobody will know where the capital ends and the Towers begins after the redevelopment."

"In the old days, when industry was concentrated in the Towers and all the other cities ringing the capital, all you had to do was look up to see where the edge was. On a calm day it was like a floating grey fortress."

"Did you hear about the deadly fog in the Seume Valley a little while back?"

"Through the grapevine."

"Your fortress seems to me more like a prison."

"I hadn't thought of it that way. People were concerned about it, though. They didn't care about what they couldn't see and were completely horrified by the pitch black smoke from the old coal plants."

The turn of the conversation has allowed her to put some distance between herself and the imminent obliteration of the Towers. She calmly sips her tea and glances regularly at the uninspired greyness of the people in the ever shorter coffee line. She doubts that any of them have wondered about the significance of the name of the cabaret and have learned about the myth. Even if the place was grim, so long as it was conveniently located between their homes and the metro station, they would likely still drink their morning coffee without comment. She is no better, not being able to recall the name of the bar the group from the office frequents after work. She starts to wonder how the families touched by the outbreak reacted to the decision.

"How did the families we visited take the news?" she asks.

"They haven't been informed. It was communicated that the source had been found, that everyone was now safe and that the government was working on a permanent solution. No specifics, no word about the classification.

"They were numb to what they heard; resigned. Nothing was going to bring their loved ones back and they had come to accept it. There was nothing to fight against and those who fought anyway were exhausted."

"Are they going to be told?"

"When everything is in place."

She accepts the response, not really caring to go further lest she inadvertently gets attached to their fate. In any case, they will probably be better off leaving this broken-down former utopia. It doesn't strike her that any of them were particularly invested in it. The building community heads would be unhappy to let go of the structure they put so much effort into, but she can imagine them being excited at the idea of putting their mark on a new one.

"What are you going to do?" she asks.

"I have a chalet in the northern mountains. The plan is to go there and do as little as possible."

"You won't be bored?"

"Bored is more pleasant than it sounds, especially after decades of managing crises and yelling matches with factory owners. You?"

"It doesn't look like I will play the role of Committee liaison anytime soon. So, back to the office, shuffling paper."

"You could request a change."

"Yeah, but I won't."

She takes her leave, thanking him for explaining what being classified as a slum meant. He stays at the table, apparently already content doing nothing. She suspects that he will be replaced with an amoeba, which will be unfortunate. Although there is no fundamental difference between the plodding ox and the insipid amoeba, having a good balance of both offers some semblance of variety. The capital and the Towers are both overrun with people like her.

Once she is outside, she looks up and down the street, expecting it to somehow look different now that it is part of a slum. Nothing has changed; the morning delivery vehicles, the steady flow of people, the stores; everything is still in its place. Most importantly, the white walls are still a brilliant, pure white that concentrates the energy of the day. If anything, she would have expected to notice the yellow-grey tinge characteristic of use, wear and eventually death. She carefully examines the wall closest to her and the only thing she comes away with is the faint smell of paint. She contemplates scraping away some of the layers, before thinking better of it. The policeman is still following her and assuaging her curiosity is not worth having petty vandalism being added to her file.

She saunters up to the main square, which is just as overpoweringly bright as the first time she saw it. She replays portions of

Andesmas's rousing discourse in her head and gets stuck on "I don't know the Towers." He was talking about the original workers utopia from which he took inspiration. He could never go back and experience the exhilaration of building such an important project as a community, a project that improved—as far as they could tell, at any rate—everyone's lives. No one will likely know if the decision to cut corners underground was out of ignorance, incompetence, greed, maliciousness or any other of a thousand reasons. Maybe the designers realized that their bright and shiny paradise would fall apart over time, so they purposefully built in a fatal weakness that would force future generations to start over and rethink the very notion of paradise. Without the crumbling foundations, it would be left as an empty shell. People would still live there, but without really living together. It is weird for her to think of utopia as temporary, though she can't think of any reason why it has to be permanent.

On the other side of the spectrum, she sees the soil problem as the result of the influence of some hippo of the time. It would not have been maliciousness so much as self-interest; better dirt and the compaction machinery were used elsewhere and not much thought was given to the consequences. It would undermine the myth of idyllic cooperation, and so fits better with her take on human nature. The associated theory is that Marne had a hand in the classification. He was not satisfied with "water" being excluded from official communications. He wanted the whole city to be blamed for the outbreak and demanded that it be wiped from the face of the earth for its role in impugning the good name of his water network. He would have also had her put in some forgotten corner of the country to live out her days isolated from society to pay for that one line in her report. If it wasn't for the same countervailing power that made the requests of Andesmas's amoeba disappear, she would already be long gone.

She enjoys the outlandishness of both theories, particularly because neither of them can be dismissed out of hand. Her train of thought falters as she realizes that she is being cooked like a sense-less tourist, slowly turning into an indistinct dark blob in the mid-dle of the plane of white. As she makes her way back to the capital, she decides to favor the first theory for the time being. The poetry she sees in the city needs to be temporary; once it is established for a long enough time—once it is implicitly assumed and no longer declared—it starts to fade away. There is an agreeable symmetry if the object of the poetry is itself just as ephemeral.

Chapter 18

The pink version of the Towers comes to the forefront as the months pass. The days are a grey and red blur, as the time in the office blends into one undifferentiated stretch. Natalie is once more convinced that Andesmas has forgotten about her and that she will have no role to play in resolving the next bizarre international crisis. Even if Andesmas's amoeba was unsuccessful at having her transferred, she can see him either endlessly repeating how unworthy she is or deleting any mention of her that comes through his office. Add that to any possible negative influence from Marne and the fact that she is just one among thousands of insipid amoebas, and there is little reason to expect another break from the bunker.

Given the experience of the Towers, she is also not entirely sure that she would care for another assignment. Her police tail has since disappeared and she no longer has to brave the personal space of random people. She received a blank postcard from New York a month ago that was obviously from George. She expected a follow-up visit from the police, but nothing happened. All interest in her seems to have vanished, along with the low-level anxiety and extravagant conspiracy theories that came with it. It would be different if she really did have useful skills. Regardless of what others might have said about her invaluable contributions, she only felt as if she were along for the ride. That is an experience she can easily do without in the future.

The files she has been analyzing have gotten thinner over time, indicating that the government has moved beyond more or less important people and is now having plans done for everyone. She, along with all her fellow open office amoebas, still manages to spend the same amount of time on each file. When the supervisor comments on it, they explain that it is more difficult to come up with ways to influence people when they have less content to work with. The second, unmentioned, difficulty is that the subjects have begun to resemble them. It is harder to suggest points of leverage when they can imagine the leverage being used on them. Despite that, the distilled essences are still more abstract than being in someone's apartment.

It is only the after-work habits that have changed. Evenings have been split evenly between the usual bar and the cabaret, one after the other. The work group has assumed that she suddenly has a family since she has started to leave the bar at the same time as those with parental responsibilities. There is mild surprise, though, since nobody ever delves very far into anyone else's private life, she has been able to go along with the mistaken impression without having to lie or correct it. The last thing she wants is for people from work to invade her other life, even if the cabaret is probably already full of amoebas just like them, so she keeps its existence to herself.

She ran into the puppeteers a couple of times at the cabaret at the outset. After she mentioned the city's new classification as a slum and explained what that meant, they accelerated their plans to establish themselves elsewhere. Unlike her, they mainly frequented the place because of its proximity to their show. So, when they found a new location, they stopped coming. She kept to herself after that, treating the experience as a joyous kind of prewake. She wanted to commune with the sort of Death who was all about excess and ignoring the pleas of the villagers, who stubbornly stayed at the bar until she had drunk her fill of local blood, who was insensible to the priest's prayers and whatever God saw fit to rain down upon her head. If anyone approached her, her apparent obsession with death and repeated demands that they buy her a pint of fermented blood made them back away quickly enough.

Death would not come to town for the bloodless demise of a city, but it was all myth and symbol anyway. Natalie can twist her into anything she wants. She might even be able to convince the proprietor of the post-redevelopment cabaret to call it the Cabaret of Four Caskets. Some owners would welcome a representation of the death of a workers utopia only possible under democracy as a subtle and practically risk-free way to challenge the Committee. For the moment, though, it is all about celebrating this alternate reality where the rules of the capital are suspended. Whether she accepts the invitation or not, Death is the guest of honor. Whether she accepts it or not, the celebration must continue with the off-kilter, anti-establishment music and the pervasive pink that frees dyed in the wool amoebas from their shades of grey.

The celebration continues for Natalie until fences are erected around the city with notices stating that the area is no longer fit for human habitation and the date that the clearing is supposed to begin. She considers climbing over the fence, but decides that there is little point to it. Instead, her after-bar habit becomes wandering around the capital to find the best vantage point to watch the beginning of the execution—the demolition of the first major buildings. The destruction of the whole city will probably take weeks or even months; watching it all seems to her needlessly masochistic.

She first explores the only major hill in the region, which is on the opposite side of the capital from the Towers. There are several viewpoint parks with shaded benches and other amenities built expressly to take in the whole region. Finding them far too distant, she works her way toward the city, looking for inclines with good sight lines. She realizes that there is no way to see the whole city, so she skips the bar for a couple of days and asks workers leaving the site where they plan to start. Armed with that information, she finds a quiet street that looks built up to match a building predating it from which she has an adequate vantage point of the demolition and is far enough away for the view to not be totally obstructed by the cloud of dust she is expecting.

The day of the event, she sits at the edge of the road at the top of the incline and leans against the building. She feels vulnerable as she blends well with the grey of the asphalt road and the concrete wall, even if all but large trucks have ample room to go around and she doubts that this is a popular street for trucks. She notices a small crowd gather at the fence; a crowd of former residents and business owners, she suspects. All the dignitaries, if there are any, are probably circled around the plunger, switch or whatever it is that sets off the explosive charges. It would be a good photo opportunity, though they will likely wait until the new city is constructed before they get into the real festivities.

"Get up."

She hears a voice behind her, turns and sees Theo, wearing his red shirt and with the blanket in his hands. After a moment of stupefaction, she obeys. He lays the blanket down for both of them and they both sit on it.

When her thoughts find the appropriate gear, she is worried that he will ask her where she has been and admonish her for abandoning him. He might go into the sad tale of how his mother never recovered from the death of Albert and how her absences now last days at a time. Maybe he will say how the loss of their home was the last straw; that she can't function anymore and had to be institutionalized. After that, he gave up on school and society, ran away from state care and became a full-time street urchin, living off the gains from his small-time burglaries. But he learned a lot in the orphanage and on the street and is ready for a bigger score, something that will set him up for a while.

She glances at him out of the corner of her eye. He seems healthy and clean, not really the profile of a street kid who has been struggling to get by. She reins in her thoughts and waits for him to say something. When nothing comes, she looks at him again; he is absorbed by the activity in the demolition site. She refocuses on that and makes an effort to pull her thoughts along. The crowd has grown larger now and everyone is completely still and silent, waiting with various levels of anticipation for the show to start.

The first explosions ring out and the row of towers directly in front of Natalie and Theo sinks to the ground in a cloud of dust. They see the tops clearly, while the crowd is encompassed by the cloud. As the dust settles, everything becomes still once again. Then, as if following a cue, the entire crowd starts brushing themselves off and commenting on the demolition. The group splits into two, with some people staying by the fence, probably judging that, since the next towers to go are farther away, they won't be engulfed again, and some, more cautious, who move back.

Natalie's first reaction is that the explosion of the nuclear bomb has finally run its course. It had been held in stasis for decades, with its intense, blinding flash and extraordinary energy concentrated in the walls of the main square and extending with diminishing power along the streets. Half of not knowing Hiroshima had to be unbelievable intensity of the detonation, the other half must have been the extent of the devastation it left behind. Now that she sees the ruins, she has a sense that it was inevitable; that there was no way of controlling that level of force indefinitely. It is also just as inadequate for truly knowing the city as any of the other ways she has seen the Towers, with the added downside of destroying any possibility that one could take inspiration from it.

She wonders where Andesmas will take the potential recruits for his common project now. While she is reflecting, the next set of detonations go off and a second line of towers sinks to the ground. The dust reaches the people still at the fence, though they are not lost in it. Suddenly, she thinks about the water treatment plant. Andesmas rehashed parts of his speech when they were leaving the plant, so maybe he would start using it for his full discourse. It lacks the energy—there would be no point for him to wear his special suit—but it is closer to his more flexible and durable model of paradise. The centrifuges and other equipment would be imposing enough to awe the prospect and make them believe that there is something much bigger than themselves, yet sufficiently concrete, that they can contribute to and feel proud of.

That could have been Marne's game all along. Making sure that his water network was above reproach may have been his original motivation for interfering in the investigation, but he is someone who thinks on a bigger scale. He would have been aware of how Andesmas was using the Towers and of the possibility that the Committee as a whole would make the city a high-profile symbol of their future plans. Andesmas was brought in because he too was a big thinker, someone capable of effectively countering the influence of the charter, so it was probably only a matter of time before he went beyond the far too rarified counter-charter and focused on something solid that people could rally around.

Marne's first move was to have the blame for the outbreak shifted from the water system to the city. Then, he invited Andesmas and her to the plant to show them how impressive it was. She was likely included in case she had some influence on Andesmas and to make sure that her reports would be careful not to include anything negative about his work. He almost shot himself in the foot with his narcissism; though, in the end, Andesmas still bought into the project as a whole. The final step was to persuade the Committee that destroying the city was the way to go, which would have been relatively easy since, as André pointed out, it was never unreasonable to begin with. Now the one development that could have overshadowed his legacy is in the middle of being destroyed. Another notch in his belt; another accomplishment to shamelessly brag about in the years to come.

Her vision of the rubble flips from a result of a nuclear bomb to that of a rampaging hippo, destroying people's homes left and right for his own personal ends, indifferent to the hardship he causes. She smiles at the absurdity of what she pictures, before the sobering implications sink in. She will never know if the theory is true. Even if there is a way to find out she isn't inclined to take the risk to do so. The damage is, in any case, done and she is less and less curious. The ruins of a city that once piqued her imagination can only interest her for so long.

She thinks about Theo, who is probably in the same situation. Now that he doesn't have the drawings of the court of Squirrel King the First on the wall in his apartment and a puppetry show around the corner, his connection to Albert must be fading. She glances at him again and notes that he appears to be taking the destruction of the city well. He is serious, not sad or angry. Maybe a boy his age is supposed to be excited by explosions and destruction, maybe normal would have been to hear him cheer and clap as the towers sunk to the ground. He might believe that he no longer has the liberty to be a kid. She doesn't know.

For her, the only thing left that sparks her imagination is the hippo, a figure that does not belong in the tedious amoeba-ox continuum that everyone else fits into. She doesn't like the idea of fixating on such a pompous and destructive creature, though. They sit on the slope, waiting for another series of detonations that does not come. After a while, she remembers that the demolition worker had said that they would only be doing the two main rows of towers today. They watch the crowd disperse without moving, neither of them having any place they are in any rush to be. Then, she has an idea that she hopes will help them both. She turns to him and says:

"Tell me about Albert's famous blue gopher."

Roundfire

FICTION

Put simply, we publish great stories. Whether it's literary or popular, a gentle tale or a pulsating thriller, the connecting theme in all Roundfire fiction titles is that once you pick them up you won't want to put them down.
If you have enjoyed this book, why not tell other readers by posting a review on your preferred book site. Recent bestsellers from Roundfire are:

The Bookseller's Sonnets
Andi Rosenthal

The Bookseller's Sonnets intertwines three love stories with a tale of religious identity and mystery spanning five hundred years and three countries.
Paperback: 978-1-84694-342-3 ebook: 978-184694-626-4

Birds of the Nile
An Egyptian Adventure
N.E. David

Ex-diplomat Michael Blake wanted a quiet birding trip up the Nile – he wasn't expecting a revolution.
Paperback: 978-1-78279-158-4 ebook: 978-1-78279-157-7

Blood Profit$
The Lithium Conspiracy
J. Victor Tomaszek, James N. Patrick, Sr.

The blood of the many for the profits of the few... Blood Profit$
will take you into the cigar-smoke-filled room where American
policy and laws are really made.
Paperback: 978-1-78279-483-7 ebook: 978-1-78279-277-2

The Burden
A Family Saga
N.E. David

Frank will do anything to keep his mother and father apart. But
he's carrying baggage – and it might just weigh him down ...
Paperback: 978-1-78279-936-8 ebook: 978-1-78279-937-5

The Cause
Roderick Vincent

The second American Revolution will be a fire lit from an
internal spark.
Paperback: 978-1-78279-763-0 ebook: 978-1-78279-762-3

Don't Drink and Fly
The Story of Bernice O'Hanlon: Part One
Cathie Devitt

Bernice is a witch living in Glasgow. She loses her way in her
life and wanders off the beaten track looking for the garden of
enlightenment.
Paperback: 978-1-78279-016-7 ebook: 978-1-78279-015-0

Gag
Melissa Unger

One rainy afternoon in a Brooklyn diner, Peter Howland punctures an egg with his fork. Repulsed, Peter pushes the plate away and never eats again.
Paperback: 978-1-78279-564-3 ebook: 978-1-78279-563-6

The Master Yeshua
The Undiscovered Gospel of Joseph
Joyce Luck

Jesus is not who you think he is. The year is 75 CE. Joseph ben Jude is frail and ailing, but he has a prophecy to fulfil ...
Paperback: 978-1-78279-974-0 ebook: 978-1-78279-975-7

On the Far Side, There's a Boy
Paula Coston

Martine Haslett, a thirty-something 1980s woman, plays hard on the fringes of the London drag club scene until one night which prompts her to sign up to a charity. She writes to a young Sri Lankan boy, with consequences far and long.
Paperback: 978-1-78279-574-2 ebook: 978-1-78279-573-5

Tuareg
Alberto Vazquez-Figueroa

With over 5 million copies sold worldwide, *Tuareg* is a classic adventure story from best-selling author Alberto Vazquez-Figueroa, about honour, revenge and a clash of cultures.
Paperback: 978-1-84694-192-4

Readers of ebooks can buy or view any of these bestsellers by clicking on the live link in the title. Most titles are published in paperback and as an ebook. Paperbacks are available in traditional bookshops. Both print and ebook formats are available online.

Find more titles and sign up to our readers' newsletter at
http://www.johnhuntpublishing.com/fiction

Follow us on Facebook at
https://www.facebook.com/JHPfiction
and Twitter at https://twitter.com/JHPFiction